The Mr Tw[...]
Stories

# The Mr Twiddle Stories

Enid Blyton

*Illustrations by Stephen Dell*

BLOOMSBURY
CHILDREN'S
BOOKS

First published by Parragon Publishing in 1999
Queen Street House, 4/5 Queen Street, Bath BA1 1HE

*Hello, Mr Twiddle!* was first published by George Newnes in 1942
First published by Bloomsbury Publishing Plc in 1997
38 Soho Square, London, W1V 5DF
*Don't Be Silly, My Twiddle!* was first published by Newnes in 1949
*Well, Really, Mr Twiddle!* was first published by George Newnes in 1953
First published by Bloomsbury Publishing Plc in 1998
38 Soho Square, London, W1V 5DF

Enid Blyton

The moral right of the author has been asserted
A CIP catalogue record of this book is available from the
British Library

ISBN 1 84164 095 6

Printed in Scotland by Caledonian International Book Manufacturing Ltd

10 9 8 7 6 5 4 3 2 1

# Contents

# Hello
# Mr Twiddle!

# Hello
# Mr Twiddle!

Enid Blyton
*Illustrations by Stephen Dell*

BLOOMSBURY
CHILDREN'S
BOOKS

# Contents

## Chapter 1
# Mr Twiddle and the Cow

One day Mrs Twiddle asked Mr Twiddle to go and fetch her brother's cow for her.

'Albert, my brother, is going away,' she said, 'and I told him we would look after his cow for a day or two, Twiddle. So you go and fetch it, and we'll keep it in the field behind the house. It will be nice to have some fresh milk for nothing.'

Mr Twiddle put down his paper and got up with a sigh. There always seemed something to do just when he was nicely settled. He brushed his hair, stuffed a clean handkerchief into his pocket, and went to the door.

'Twiddle, don't forget your hat,' said Mrs Twiddle. 'I believe you'd forget to take your head with you if it wasn't so firmly fixed on.'

'I don't want my hat,' said Mr Twiddle.

'You *must* take your hat!' said Mrs Twiddle firmly. 'The sun is going to be hot.'

So Twiddle had to take his hat. But he felt rather obstinate that morning and he made up his mind that although he had to take his hat, he wouldn't wear it. No, he'd carry it in his hand! Aha, Mrs Twiddle, you'd be cross if you saw that!

It was a nice hat, for it was a new one. It was brown, and had a fine brown ribbon round it, tied in a bow at the side. It fitted Mr Twiddle perfectly. Secretly Mr Twiddle thought he looked extremely nice in his new hat, and he quite meant to put it on if he met anyone. But he didn't.

He got to the field and called the cow. The cow, a gentle creature who knew him well, came to the gate at once. Mr Twiddle tied a rope round her neck and led her off.

He hadn't gone far before his shoelace came undone. Mr Twiddle looked down at it. He had his hat in one hand and the cow's rope in the other. What was he to do?

'I must just hang my hat up somewhere,' said Mr Twiddle, in a dreamy voice, for he was hot and rather sleepy. He looked for something to hang his hat up on, and saw the cow's horns, looking just like the hall pegs at home on which he always hung his hat.

Mr Twiddle put his hat on the horns of the surprised cow. Then he knelt down and did up his shoelace, very cleverly, with one hand.

'Ha!' he said proudly, when he had finished. 'Some folks may call me a stupid man – but it isn't many who could tie a lace with one hand!'

He walked on with the cow, feeling quite

pleased with himself. The cow came gently after him, wearing the brown hat, looking very comical indeed. But Mr Twiddle had forgotten all about his hat.

It wasn't until the sun shone down really hotly on his head that he felt he needed a hat. He put his hand up to his head and found no hat there. He looked at his two hands. Now what had happened to his hat? He had certainly started out with it!

'Oh, bother, bother, bother!' said Mr Twiddle. 'I must have left it on the gate where I fetched the cow!'

So back he went, the cow still following, Mr Twiddle's hat perched up on her horns. Soon they met Mrs Gabble, and how she laughed to see the cow!

'Sorry I can't raise my hat to you this morning,' said Mr Twiddle politely, 'but I've put it somewhere and forgotten it!'

'Ho, ho, so you have!' giggled Mrs Gabble, and she laughed till the tears ran down her cheek.

The next person Mr Twiddle met was Dame Shoo, and she looked quite alarmed when she saw Mr Twiddle without a hat and the cow with one.

'Just going to look for my hat, Dame Shoo,' said Mr Twiddle politely. 'You know, I've left it somewhere about, and I must find it.'

'Ask the cow and maybe she'll tell you where it is,' said Dame Shoo with a squeal of laughter.

Mr Twiddle looked crossly at her. 'Silly woman!' he thought. 'Ask the cow indeed! As if *she* could tell me where my hat is!'

Then he met Mr Wonks, the hot-sausage man who sold ice-creams in the summer.

'Good day, Mr Twiddle!' said Mr Wonks, grinning at the cow. 'Hot weather for the cow, isn't it! I see you don't want her to get a headache.'

Mr Twiddle stared at him in amazement. What *could* Mr Wonks mean?

'You must be mad, Mr Wonks,' said Mr Twiddle, in a high and mighty voice. 'Cows don't get headaches.'

'No, nor sunstroke either, by the look of things!' grinned Mr Wonks.

Mr Twiddle said no more. He began to think that the sun had made everyone a little mad this morning. He got to the field gate, but alas! there was no hat to be seen. Mr

Twiddle was upset. Someone must have been along and taken it!

'My nice new hat too!' he said mournfully. 'What, oh what, will Mrs Twiddle say?'

He went home so upset that he didn't notice how everyone laughed at the cow with the hat on. He took the cow round to the back door, to show Mrs Twiddle, for she was fond of the gentle creature.

As soon as Mrs Twiddle opened the door, Mr Twiddle began to explain about his hat.

'I'm so very sorry,' he said, 'but somehow or other I seem to have lost my hat. Maybe it blew away – maybe someone stole it – I don't know what happened. But, anyway, I'm very sorry, my dear, and I'll go and buy a new one this very minute. I do wish I knew what had happened to it.'

'If you look behind you, you'll see that the cow had more sense than you,' cried his wife. 'She knew how to bring a hat home, anyhow!'

Twiddle turned and looked at the cow. He saw his hat perched on her horns. The cow opened her mouth and spoke gently.

'Moo-oo!' she said, 'moo-oo!' And she waggled her head gently, asking Mr Twiddle to take off the hat, for it annoyed her.

'Oh, the clever creature!' cried Mr Twiddle, in the greatest delight. 'Mrs Twiddle, do you see, she has got my hat for me! She must have found it and put it on, and brought it all the way home for me! Now isn't that really remarkably clever? I must go and tell everyone about this most extraordinary cow.'

And with that Mr Twiddle beamed all over his face, gave his wife a good slap and kissed the cow on the nose.

'Sorry, dear, sorry!' he said, as he saw Mrs Twiddle looking as black as thunder. 'I meant to kiss you and slap the cow, I did really!'

And, clapping his hat on his head upside down, he hurried off to tell everyone the story of how the cow had found his hat and worn it home. Dear old Twiddle, he *is* a muddler, isn't he!

## Chapter 2
# Mr Twiddle Gets a Shock

Mr Twiddle was always doing something silly. Well, did you ever hear the tale of what happened when he threw his handkerchief into the fire by mistake?

I'll tell you. It happened one morning when Mr Twiddle was opening his letters by the kitchen fire. 'You can throw the envelopes into the fire,' said Mrs Twiddle. 'It will save me fetching the waste-paper basket.'

Well, Mr Twiddle at that moment felt he was going to sneeze, so, with an envelope in one hand and his best white silk handkerchief in the other, he sat in his chair, waiting for the sneeze to come.

And when it *did* come – a-TISH-oo-ish-oo!

– Mr Twiddle caught the sneeze in the envelope, and threw his handkerchief, quite by mistake, into the fire!

Well, of course, he was terribly upset as soon as he had done this, and tried to rake his handkerchief out of the fire. A bit of burning coal fell on the rug and scorched a hole at once. Mrs Twiddle came running in when she smelt the smell of burning – and how she scolded Mr Twiddle!

'Catching a sneeze in an envelope and throwing your best handkerchief on the fire!' she snorted, pouring water on the burning rug. 'Whatever will you do next, Twiddle? Don't you know the difference between a handkerchief and an envelope? You'll be poking the fire with your pencil and trying to write with the poker next! You might have had the whole house on fire. Go out for a walk, do, and don't come in till dinner time!'

Poor Mr Twiddle! He was really very unhappy about his best handkerchief. He got up, found his hat, put it on back to front and went into the village. And very soon he met old Mrs Gabble, who always loved a chat. When she saw Mr Twiddle looking so upset, she stopped.

'What's the matter?' she said.

'Oh,' said Mr Twiddle, 'a dreadful thing happened this morning. I threw my handkerchief on the fire by mistake, and it got burnt, and when I tried to get it out of the flames, some burning coal fell on the carpet and . . .'

'Good gracious me!' said Mrs Gabble, 'no wonder you felt upset!' Then she caught sight of Sally Simple and she hurried to tell her the news. But, of course, she added a bit to it to make it even more exciting!

'Oh, Sally Simple,' she cried, 'have you heard what happened at the Twiddles' house this morning? Why, poor old Twiddle threw his handkerchief on the fire by mistake and, in getting it out, the fire fell on to the rug and set it all ablaze!'

'Goodness me!' said Sally, quite frightened. 'And did the kitchen catch alight?'

'I expect so,' said Mrs Gabble happily. 'Oh yes, I am sure it blazed up on to the ceiling!'

Sally Simple was thrilled. She longed to tell someone about the fire at the Twiddles'. She saw Dame Shoo over the way and rushed to tell her.

'Oh, Dame Shoo,' she cried, 'have you heard of the terrible fire at poor Mrs Twiddle's this morning?'

'No,' said Dame Shoo, startled. 'What about it?'

'Oh, Mr Twiddle dropped his handkerchief in the fire, and that started a dreadful burning,' said Sally Simple. 'Yes, the rug caught fire, and the flames shot up to the ceiling! The whole kitchen was on fire.'

'But how dreadful!' said Dame Shoo. 'I

suppose the house will be burnt down?'

'Yes, sure to be,' said Sally Simple. 'I do wonder if the fire engines have gone to see to it. And don't you think we ought to offer to give the Twiddles a bed for tonight, because, with their house burnt down, they'll have nowhere to sleep?'

'Yes, yes!' said Dame Shoo. 'I'll go and tell everyone else, Sally, and we'll see what we can do.'

She hurried off, longing to tell someone the news.

On the way she passed the fire station. She peeped inside – and to her very great surprise she saw the big fire engine still there. It hadn't gone to the Twiddles'!

'I say! I say!' cried Dame Shoo, rushing into the fire station in a great hurry. 'Haven't you heard of the dreadful fire at the Twiddles' house? It will be burnt to nothing if you don't hurry at once!'

'First we've heard of it!' cried the captain of the fire brigade, and he sounded the big fire bell at once.

In three minutes every fireman was in his place, complete with helmet. With a loud clanging of bells the great red fire engine roared out of the building.

Clang! Clang! Clang! It sped away to Mr Twiddle's house. Everyone ran after it to see where it was going. It stopped outside Mr Twiddle's house. The firemen undid the long hose and looked for the fire.

Mrs Twiddle looked out of the window. She saw the fire engine. She saw the firemen unwinding the hose. She saw the crowds and crowds of people. Whatever had they all come for?

She opened the door and looked out.

'Hie, Mrs Twiddle, where's the fire?' shouted the men.

'What fire?' asked Mrs Twiddle, in the greatest astonishment.

'The fire we've come to put out!' said the men.

'Well, there's only one fire in the house and that's in the kitchen grate,' said Mrs Twiddle, even more astonished. 'And I'm sure I don't want *that* put out, thank you!'

At that moment Mr Twiddle walked up, looking as surprised as could be to see such a crowd round his house.

'You said there was a terrible fire in your house!' cried Dame Shoo.

'I didn't!' said Mr Twiddle indignantly.

'You did!' shouted everyone.

'I only told Mrs Gabble I had burnt my handkerchief by mistake!' shouted Mr Twiddle, and he went inside and banged the door.

The fire engine turned round and drove off in disgust. Everyone went home. Mrs Twiddle stared at Mr Twiddle crossly.

'Do you need to bring the fire engine here and half the town, just because you happen to have burnt your handkerchief?' she said. 'Really, Mr Twiddle! Please don't do any more foolish things today.'

'Don't worry, I *shan't*!' said Mr Twiddle gloomily, and he threw his hat into the waste-paper basket and hung up his newspaper on a peg.

Well, really, Mr Twiddle!

## Chapter 3

# Mr Twiddle Fetches the Fish

'Mr Twiddle, Mr Twiddle, the fish boy hasn't been with the fish!' called Mrs Twiddle. 'Just put on your coat and go and fetch it for me, will you! And you might get the newspaper at the same time, because it hasn't been left this morning.'

Mr Twiddle jumped up at once. He had missed his newspaper very much, and he was pleased to go and fetch it. Yes, he would fetch the fish as well – it was on the way to the newspaper shop.

He went off, humming, looking forward to a nice lazy morning with his newspaper when he got back. Ah, there was nothing like a good fat newspaper and a nice brown pipe! Mrs Twiddle would be pleased with him for fetching the fish, and would let him read in peace.

He came to the fish shop and called the man. 'Can I have Mrs Twiddle's fish, please?' he asked. 'It hasn't come.'

'Certainly, sir, certainly,' said the man. 'Five herrings, isn't it? Here they are!'

He took a newspaper, slapped the five slippery herrings into it, and rolled them up. He gave the parcel to Mr Twiddle, who slipped it under his arm. He set off to the newspaper shop.

'My newspaper, please,' he said to the man. 'You forgot to leave it this morning.'

'Sorry, sir!' said the man, and he rolled up Mr Twiddle's newspaper and gave it to him. Mr Twiddle put it under his other arm.

Then he set off home, whistling softly. Ah, it would be nice to sit down in his armchair by the fire, unfold his newspaper, light his pipe, and puff away in peace, whilst Mrs Twiddle cooked herrings, and he smelt the delicious smell of them!

He reached home, and slapped down his newspaper on the table. 'Fish, Mrs Twiddle, fish!' he said. 'Good fat herrings for dinner!'

He didn't notice that he had put his newspaper on the table, and had put the parcel of fish on his chair. The fish was wrapped in a newspaper too, so it wasn't a difficult mistake to make.

Mr Twiddle went to get his pipe. Mrs Twiddle unrolled the newspaper he had put on the table. She looked astonished, and then called to Mr Twiddle: 'Twiddle! What have you done with the fish? It isn't here!'

'Isn't there!' said Twiddle in alarm. 'But it must be! I saw the man slap the herrings into the paper myself!'

'Then they must have dropped out, Mr Twiddle,' said Mrs Twiddle crossly. 'Just like you! You'd better go back and get some more.'

Mr Twiddle stared in dismay. 'But I want to read and to smoke my pipe!' he said. 'I'm tired!'

'Well, sit down for five minutes and rest,' said Mrs Twiddle. 'Then you must go, or we will have nothing for dinner.'

Twiddle sighed. Something always seemed to go wrong. He looked for his newspaper. Ah yes, he had put it in his armchair. The cat was there too, scraping hard at the paper. It could smell the fish in it, of course! But Mr Twiddle didn't know that. He thought it was just his newspaper and nothing else.

'Look at the cat!' he said to his wife. 'I believe she's trying to open the newspaper and read it!'

'Fiddlesticks!' said Mrs Twiddle snappily.

'Whatever will you say next? You'll tell me the canary wants to smoke your pipe!'

Mr Twiddle lit his pipe. Then he took up the newspaper from the chair and sat down. He shook out the paper – and out fell five slippery herrings, all down Mr Twiddle's nice clean waistcoat and trousers!

'Bless us all, what's this!' shouted Mr Twiddle in a fright, jumping up. 'Mrs Twiddle, Mrs Twiddle, there's something hiding in my newspaper – big earwigs, or something! Ooo-ooo-oooh! They all jumped out at me when I opened my paper!'

The cat jumped at the fish in delight. She sat down and began to eat. Mr Twiddle beamed at her.

'Look at that now!' he cried. 'The cat's attacking them! Clever creature!'

Mrs Twiddle hurried in and gave a shout of dismay. 'It's the herrings!' she cried. 'Twiddle, are you mad? What have you given them to the cat for? Shoo, puss, shoo!'

The cat shooed. Mr Twiddle looked foolish. Mrs Twiddle picked up the herrings, scolding all the while.

'Really, what shall I do with you, Twiddle! Giving me your newspaper, and trying to read the herrings, and then giving them to the cat! Well, there will be one less for your dinner now, for the cat's had one.'

'I did *not* give them to the cat,' said Mr Twiddle crossly.

'You did!' said Mrs Twiddle. 'Didn't I see you beaming at the cat eating the herrings when I came in?'

'Well,' said Mr Twiddle, cheering up suddenly, 'I needn't go off to the fish shop again, because the fish are found. So I can read my newspaper in peace! Where is it?'

'Oh, I've torn it up to make new paper to line the larder shelves,' said Mrs Twiddle. 'If you want to read it you'll have to go and stand in the larder and read the news on each shelf, Mr Twiddle. That will teach you to give herrings to that cat again!'

Poor Twiddle! He spent all the morning in the larder, reading the news on each shelf, for Mrs Twiddle had torn up the paper and spread it neatly there. He couldn't even have his pipe, for he wasn't allowed to smoke one in the larder. He really is the funniest old thing, isn't he!

## Chapter 4
# Mr Twiddle and
# the Snowman

One day the children who lived next door to Mr Twiddle made a fine snowman in his garden. Mrs Twiddle said they might, because her garden was so much bigger than theirs. So the children were very pleased, and they built a big man, quite as tall as their daddy, and very fat and round.

'Mrs Twiddle, Mrs Twiddle, can we have an old hat for his head, and an old scarf for his neck?' called the children, looking in at the kitchen window, where Mrs Twiddle was making cakes.

'Yes,' said Mrs Twiddle. 'You'll find an old hat in the hall, and a ragged old scarf somewhere by it. And if you look in the hall drawer you'll maybe find an old pair of gloves too, for the snowman's cold hands!'

'Oh, good!' shouted the children, and they tore off to get the clothes. They found them all – and they found Mr Twiddle's stick too, which they borrowed for their funny old snowman.

My word, he did look grand when he was finished and dressed up! You should have seen him, with Mr Twiddle's old hat on his head, a scarf tied loosely round his fat neck, raggedy gloves on his round hands, and a stick through his arm! Really, he looked very fine indeed, and the children were proud of him.

Mrs Twiddle looked out of the window and laughed. 'He just wants a pipe to stick in his mouth,' she said, 'then he'll be happy. Here is one of Mr Twiddle's.'

So the children stuck a pipe in the snowman's mouth, and then danced round him, laughing. Their mother called them in for tea next door, and they hurried off, hungry and happy, wondering what Mr Twiddle would say when he saw their wonderful snowman.

Well, Mr Twiddle didn't come home till it was almost dark, for he had been to see his brother in the next village. He stumped in at the front gate, tired and hungry – and then he suddenly saw the old snowman standing quite still in his front garden.

'Hello!' said Mr Twiddle, in surprise. 'Who's that? What are you doing here, my good man?'

The good man didn't answer. Mr Twiddle grew cross.

'You needn't think I can't see you, standing there, trying to hide from me in the darkness!' he said. 'You are up to no good, I'll be bound! What are you waiting there for?'

The snowman said nothing at all. Mr Twiddle marched right up to him and looked at him as closely as he could in the half-darkness. And he saw that the snowman had got *his* hat on!

'You've got my hat!' he said, in a rage. 'My dear old comfortable hat! How dare you take my hat! Give it to me at once!'

The snowman didn't give it to Mr Twiddle. He just stood quite still and stared at him out of his big stone eyes.

'And you've got my scarf on, I do declare!' roared Mr Twiddle. 'Yes, you have! What next, I'd like to know! I suppose you've been sneaking round my house, just taking whatever you can put your hands on! I'll fetch a policeman!'

The snowman stared and said nothing. 'Can't you answer me?' shouted Mr Twiddle. 'Haven't you got a tongue in your head?'

The poor old snowman hadn't got a tongue of any sort, so he couldn't say a word. He just stood there in Mr Twiddle's hat and scarf, looking very large and miserable.

'And if you haven't got my gloves and my stick!' cried Mr Twiddle, suddenly seeing them in darkness, and feeling them. 'This is too much! My hat, my scarf – and now my gloves and my stick! You are a wicked robber, and if you don't give me back my things at once, this very minute, I'll go out and get a policeman! Now!'

The snowman didn't move. Then a bit of snow melted by his mouth and his pipe fell out. Mr Twiddle picked it up.

'And you've got my pipe too!' he shouted. 'My very nicest, oldest pipe! What next! Are you wearing my vests and my socks and my best shirt under that large white overcoat of yours? Oh, you bad, wicked robber!'

Just then the village policeman came by and heard the shouting. He walked into the front garden.

'Now then, what's all this?' he asked.

'Oh, policeman, I'm glad you've come,' said Mr Twiddle. 'This robber won't give me back my clothes that he's stolen. He must be deaf and dumb, for he won't even say a word to me.'

Mr Twiddle suddenly slipped on the snow and fell against the snowman. He clutched at him and one of the snowman's stone buttons fell off and hit Mr Twiddle sharply on the nose.

'Oh, you wicked fellow, you hit me!' shouted Mr Twiddle in a rage. 'Take that – and that – and that!'

He slapped the snowman hard, and the snow fell off in big pieces. Mr Twiddle was astonished. He hit the snowman again, and the funny old snowman began to fall to bits. Mr Twiddle fell on top of him and floundered about in the snow, shouting and smacking. The policeman pulled him up, just as Mrs Twiddle came to the door in astonishment, to see what was the matter.

'Twiddle! What are you doing?' she called. 'Are you being rude to the policeman?'

'No, Mam, he isn't,' said the policeman, with a grin. 'He's fighting a big snowman and breaking him all to bits!'

'Really, Mr Twiddle!' said Mrs Twiddle, in surprise. '*Must* you do a thing like that? And look at the mess you're in! Good gracious me – and you've spoilt your new hat and broken your nice new stick! Well, you'll have to use your old ones again. The snowman has got them, so you can bring them in with you before he melts all over them.'

Poor Mr Twiddle! He couldn't think of a word to say – not a word! He went into the kitchen, all covered with snow, and Mrs Twiddle shooed him out again.

'I'm not going to let you cover my nice kitchen floor with melting snow!' she cried. 'Shake yourself in the yard, please! And chop up your broken stick – it will do for firewood!'

Mr Twiddle went to the woodshed very gloomily. He took the chopper – and, oh dear me, he chopped up his hat, and then went to hang his broken stick on the peg! There really is no knowing what he'll do next!

## Chapter 5
# Mr Twiddle Makes a Muddle

Once upon a time Mrs Twiddle got very tired of having Mr Twiddle in the house.

'Mr Twiddle, for goodness' sake go out into the garden and do some work!' she cried. 'Do you know what you've been doing all the morning? You've been trying to smoke your fountain pen, and you've put your pipe into the inkstand! And is it you who has stood the poker in the hall stand and put your umbrella in the fender?'

'Oh dear! Oh dear!' said Mr Twiddle, taking his fountain pen out of his mouth and staring at it. 'I thought my pipe tasted a bit funny today. I'll go out and do a bit of gardening, Mrs Twiddle.'

'You'd better, before you start to poke the fire with your umbrella,' said Mrs Twiddle. 'Your best one, too! Really, Twiddle, why don't you use your brains?'

Mr Twiddle could hear by the way that his wife talked that she was not in a very good temper. So he quickly went into the hall, put on his boots, tied his old scarf round his neck, and ran out of doors.

It was cold. What should he do? He poked his head into the shed. It was dark there, but he could see something piled up in a corner.

'Bless us all!' said Mr Twiddle, staring. 'I believe those are daffodil bulbs we've forgotten to plant. Dear, dear! – what would Mrs Twiddle say if she knew all those were sprouting away there in the corner, instead of growing into nice yellow daffodils for the spring? Now, it would be a good thing if I planted them all. That would keep me busy all the morning.'

So he took his spade and set to work. He dug up the bed, and then fetched the bulbs in his barrow. He set them all in nice rows, and covered them up gently with earth. Oh, he could work well when he liked, could Mr Twiddle. He quite enjoyed himself, for the morning was fine.

He planted every single bulb, and then he heard his wife calling him.

'You seem to be working very hard, Mr Twiddle. I suppose you will be hungry for dinner. Would you like a nice stew with carrots and onions and turnips?'

'Oooh, yes!' said Mr Twiddle, feeling quite hungry at the thought.

'Well, fetch me a few carrots, one large turnip, and some onions from the shed,' called Mrs Twiddle. So Mr Twiddle went to the shed and looked round. The carrots were in a basket, and so were a few turnips. He put them into a box and looked round for the onions. He couldn't see a single one. He trotted back to the house.

'There are no onions at all,' he said.

'Rubbish!' said Mrs Twiddle. 'There are heaps. Go back and look again, Twiddle.'

So Mr Twiddle went back and looked again. But still he couldn't see any onions, although this time he looked up at the roof of the shed too, thinking they might be hung there. He trotted back to the house again.

'I'm sorry, Mrs Twiddle, but really and truly there are no onions there!' he said.

'Mr Twiddle, you make me cross!' said Mrs Twiddle. 'Why, I put the onions in the shed myself! I'll come and show you. Really, I should have thought you knew an onion by now.'

Mrs Twiddle went down to the shed with Mr Twiddle.

She looked all round – and then she stared in surprise.

'How strange!' she said. 'How very, very strange! Not a single onion here! Where have they all gone? You haven't been eating them, Twiddle, have you?'

'Of course not,' said Mr Twiddle, offended. 'I don't eat raw onions. Whereabouts did you put them?'

'In that corner,' said Mrs Twiddle, pointing. 'They were there yesterday – a whole heap of them. Wherever can they have gone to?'

Mr Twiddle stared at the corner where his wife was pointing – and a horrid cold feeling came over him. There *had* been something in that corner this morning – and he had planted it – dozens and dozens and dozens!

'What are you looking like that for, Mr Twiddle?' asked Mrs Twiddle, staring at him. 'Have you done something to my onions?'

'Nothing very much, dear,' said Mr Twiddle, trying to smile. 'I – well – I just planted them all, that's all!'

'*Planted* them, Twiddle!' said Mrs Twiddle, in the greatest surprise. 'What did you want to plant onions for? You helped me yourself to pull them up from the ground in the autumn! Why did you plant them again?'

'I thought they were bulbs,' said Mr Twiddle.

'Well, they *are* bulbs!' said Mrs Twiddle,

'but they are not the sort to plant in the garden.'

'I thought they were daffodils,' said poor Mr Twiddle. 'I've been very, very hard at work all the morning, planting them in neat rows. I thought it would be such a surprise for you.'

'Well, it certainly *is* a surprise,' said Mrs Twiddle. 'And now, Twiddle, I'm afraid if you want any onions in your stew for dinner, you'll have to do some more hard work and dig up those onions again!'

Poor Mr Twiddle. He sadly took up his spade and dug up all the dozens and dozens and dozens of onions he had so carefully planted that morning! And wasn't he hungry when he had finished! 'I could eat two whole stews, I declare!' he said to Mrs Twiddle, when he went in.

There was a beautiful stew for him, and he did enjoy it.

'I'm sorry you had your work all for nothing, Twiddle,' said Mrs Twiddle, as she gave him a fourth helping of the stew. 'But, my dear man, do try and think what you're doing in future.'

'Oh, I will, Mrs Twiddle, I will!' said Mr

Twiddle, picking up the sugar-sifter and shaking sugar all over his stew instead of pepper. 'I've quite made up my mind about that!'

And he stirred his lemonade with the salt spoon, smiling all over his funny old face! You just can't stop him from doing things like that, can you!

## Chapter 6
# Mr Twiddle in the Rain

Once Mr Twiddle wanted to go and call on a friend of his and borrow a book. So he knocked out his pipe, put down his newspaper, and got up.

'Where are you going, Twiddle?' asked Mrs Twiddle.

'I'm going to Mr Twisty's,' said Mr Twiddle. 'He's got a most exciting book I want to borrow – all about pirates.'

'But it's pouring with rain, Twiddle!' said Mrs Twiddle. 'You'll get soaked!'

'Oh no, I'll put on my mackintosh and take my umbrella,' said Twiddle. 'I shall be all right.'

He went into the hall, thinking about the book of pirates. He took down his mackintosh and put it on. He wasn't thinking at all of what he was doing, and when he saw his coat hanging on its usual peg, he put that on, too, over his mackintosh. Then he hunted for his umbrella.

There it was in the umbrella stand. Good! Mr Twiddle took it out. He went to the front door and put up his umbrella. He walked down the path – but he had got no further than the front gate when he heard Mrs Twiddle knocking on the window.

'What do you want?' shouted Twiddle.

'You want your *mackintosh* on!' shouted Mrs Twiddle. 'You said you would put it on. Come and do so!'

Mr Twiddle stared down at himself in astonishment. 'But I did put it on!' he called back.

'Twiddle, don't be silly,' said Mrs Twiddle, and she hurried to the front door and opened it. 'Come back at once. You can see quite well you've got your overcoat on. What's the use of a mac if you don't use it when it's raining?'

Twiddle walked back, shut his umbrella, and looked for his mackintosh. Of course, as he already had it on under his coat, it was nowhere to be found.

'Well!' said Twiddle in amazement, 'it was certainly hanging on its peg in the hall when I came out of the kitchen just now. Where's it gone?'

'Mackintoshes can't walk,' said Mrs Twiddle, busy looking everywhere. 'Now where in the world have you put that mackintosh, Mr Twiddle?'

Well, Mr and Mrs Twiddle hunted everywhere. Twiddle went upstairs into his bedroom and took everything out of his wardrobe. Then he went downstairs and out into the gardener's shed to see if by any chance he had left it there.

And whilst he was there he hung his umbrella up on a peg with all the spades and forks. But he couldn't find his mackintosh. So indoors he went again, leaving his umbrella out in the shed.

When he got indoors he wanted to use his handkerchief to catch a sneeze in. So he undid his coat and tried to find his trousers pocket – but, of course, his mackintosh was underneath and he couldn't seem to get to his pocket at all.

Mrs Twiddle looked to see what he was

struggling about – and saw his mackintosh
under his coat!

'Twiddle!' she cried. 'If you aren't the
most tiresome man under the sun! *There's*
your mackintosh!'

'Where?' asked Twiddle, looking all round
him and up on the ceiling too, as if he
expected to see it flying around.

'On your own self!' cried Mrs Twiddle.

'You put it on – and then put your coat over it! Good gracious, I do believe you'll forget your own head one day and go walking off without it!'

'Well, my dear, you needn't say any more,' said Twiddle. 'It was just a mistake. After all, this hall is so dark that it's not to be wondered at if I put my mac on first and then my coat. Well, I'll go. It's still raining very hard, so I'll take off my coat and just have my mac on.'

'And what about your umbrella?' asked Mrs Twiddle, looking in the umbrella stand. 'Where's that gone now? You had it over your arm a few minutes ago.'

'Oh, it's about somewhere,' said Twiddle, looking round anxiously. Really, it was most extraordinary the way his things seemed to vanish! That umbrella was really nowhere to be seen!

'Well, I can't waste all my morning getting you ready to go out into the rain,' said Mrs Twiddle. 'I've got to peel some potatoes for dinner.'

She left Twiddle standing in the hall, looking everywhere for his lost umbrella. She took a basket and went out to the shed for some potatoes.

Mrs Twiddle filled her basket, and was just going out of the shed when she happened to look up – and she caught sight of Twiddle's umbrella hanging on a peg beside a spade and a fork. She stared at it in the greatest surprise. Then she went quickly into the house.

'Twiddle! Twiddle!' she called. 'You must have thought your umbrella was a rake or a hoe! You've hung it up with the tools in the shed!'

Well, really! Poor Mr Twiddle! He stared at Mrs Twiddle as if he couldn't believe his ears. Then, very red indeed, he went to the shed to get his umbrella. He came back with it.

He had made up his mind to be really sensible now. He would even put on his boots!

So he hunted for them and put them on. He did up his mac. He put up his umbrella and set off down the path just as the clock was striking one.

Mrs Twiddle called to him. 'Twiddle! Can't you see that the sun is shining hotly now and that the rain is over? You *do* look foolish in your mac and boots and umbrella! Also, don't you want any lunch? It's one o'clock, and I've just put it on the table!'

'Dear, dear! I've got to go without that pirate book!' groaned Twiddle. And he hung his boots on his coat peg, stuck his mac into the umbrella stand, and put his umbrella into the boot cupboard. Do you suppose he *ever* thinks what he is doing?

## Chapter 7
# Mr Twiddle's Bonfires

Guy Fawkes Day was coming near. Mr Twiddle stopped and looked each morning in the toy shop, which had a wonderful show of brightly coloured fireworks in the window.

Now Mr Twiddle loved fireworks – but Mrs Twiddle didn't. She said they were noisy, bangy things that left a lot of rubbish behind them in the garden. So for many years Mr Twiddle had had to listen to other people's fireworks, and hadn't had any of his own.

But this year he had a good idea. He would buy some for the children next door! Ah, that really *was* a fine idea! Then Mr Twiddle could look out of the window and see the children letting off the fireworks –

and it would be as good as setting them off himself!

So on Bonfire Day he went to the toy shop and bought a fine collection. There were six rockets, four Roman candles, any amount of squibs, four large catherine wheels, and a great many little odd fireworks that he didn't know the name of. The man put them into a big paper bag and gave them to Mr Twiddle.

When he got home he found that Mrs Twiddle had put on her gardening boots and coat, and was going down the garden.

'Oh, there you are, Twiddle,' she said. 'Put on your gardening boots too, and come along with me. It's quite time we took down the old beanpoles and sweet-pea sticks and burnt them all, along with the other rubbish. It's a fine afternoon, so it will do us good.'

'Right,' said Twiddle, and he put on his old boots. He went down the garden, carrying his bag of fireworks, for he meant to hand them over the fence to the children when he saw them. He popped them into his wheelbarrow, and went to fetch his fork.

Mr and Mrs Twiddle worked hard. They took up all the old poles and sticks, put aside those that would do for another year, and threw the others on to the bonfire. What a lot of rubbish there was! Old stems of cut-down plants, rotten potatoes, bad apples – oh, a heap of things that badly needed burning.

'If there's one thing I do like,' said Mr Twiddle, building up the rubbish heap, 'it's a good bonfire!'

He pushed a sheet of newspaper at the bottom of the heap and set alight to it. It flared up and the bonfire began to burn merrily, for Mr Twiddle really was good at getting bonfires going. He leaned on his fork and watched the fire.

Soon it began to die down. Mr Twiddle called to his wife: 'Bring some more rubbish. It wants feeding a little.'

Mrs Twiddle piled some old sticks into the wheelbarrow and wheeled it to the fire. She tipped the barrow over and everything went on to the burning heap. Mr Twiddle forked it into the heart of the bonfire.

'That's fine,' he said, pleased. 'My word, wife, hark at the crackling!'

But there was soon something else to listen to besides the crackling! For Mrs Twiddle had emptied the bag of fireworks on to the bonfire too! Right into the heart of the fire they went, and Twiddle forked them well in, not knowing that they were his precious fireworks.

The flames caught hold of them. They burnt a rocket. BANG! Whooooooosh! The rocket flew out of the bonfire like an aeroplane and took Mrs Twiddle's hat off. She gasped and screamed.

'Twiddle! What was that? Oh, what was that?'

A shower of stars showed up at the end of the garden. It was the end of the rocket. Then BANG! Another one went off, and shot out of the fire between Twiddle's legs, knocking away his fork as it went.

'Oooooh!' said Twiddle in the greatest surprise. He jumped well away quickly as another rocket soared over his back, showering him with coloured stars!

The catherine wheels spluttered and fizzed. The Roman candles exploded with a roar. The squibs and other little fireworks went off bang and jumped out of the flames as if they were alive!

'Save us! What's all this?' screamed poor Mrs Twiddle, jumping out of the way of a firework that seemed to want to hop on her toes all the time. 'Ow! Get away, you horrid thing! Oh, there it is again! *Will* you get away?'

Twiddle stared in surprise at the bonfire. Then he suddenly guessed what had happened. Mrs Twiddle had emptied his fireworks on the fire!

'Oh, you threw all the fireworks I bought for the children next door on to the bonfire!' he cried. 'You silly woman!'

'Silly woman, indeed!' said Mrs Tiddle angrily. 'Why didn't you tell me you had got fireworks in your barrow? Silly man! Very, very silly man!'

'Well, I must buy some more for the children,' said Twiddle, jumping out of the way
of a rocket. 'I'm tired of this. I'm going in.'

'Twiddle, just listen to *me*,' said Mrs
Twiddle firmly. 'You are *not* going to waste
your money on any more fireworks. As likely
as not you'll throw them into the kitchen fire
and then there'd be a fine to-do! Not

another penny are you to spend on fire-works. Do you hear?'

'Very well,' said Twiddle meekly. He was very sad as he went indoors. Now he wouldn't be able to see any fireworks after all.

But cheer up, Mr Twiddle! The children have bought plenty for themselves, and if only you go upstairs to your bedroom window, you'll see them all! So cheer up, Mr Twiddle.

## Chapter 8
# Mr Twiddle's Mistake

At ten o'clock every night Mr Twiddle let in the cat, and took the dog out to his kennel. If he ever forgot, Mrs Twiddle always reminded him. The cat was usually waiting outside to come in, and the dog was usually quite ready to go out to his nice cosy kennel, lined with warm straw.

One night, at ten o'clock, Mrs Twiddle looked at Mr Twiddle. He was fast asleep in his chair, his head nodding over his book.

'Twiddle!' said Mrs Twiddle sharply. 'Wake up! It's ten o'clock. Time for BED.'

'Ooooomph!' said Mr Twiddle, opening his eyes with a jerk. 'Er – what did you say, my dear? I wasn't asleep.'

'Oh yes you were, Twiddle,' said his wife,

folding up her knitting. 'Come along now. It's ten.'

So up they went to bed, Mr Twiddle still feeling very sleepy. He quite forgot about the dog and the cat. But Mrs Twiddle remembered.

'Twiddle! Have you let the cat in? And what about the dog?'

'Bother!' said Twiddle sleepily, putting his coat on once more. 'Well, I'll go down again.'

Down he went into the dark hall. He whistled to the dog to come to him. Then he opened the door. It was quite dark outside. Twiddle felt an animal against his legs and he thought it was the dog. But it wasn't. The dog was lying on the couch, feeling rather guilty because he hadn't answered Mr Twiddle's whistle and gone to him. But he felt as if he would rather sleep indoors that night, because it was cold.

It was the cat that Mr Twiddle had felt! It had come indoors and rubbed against his legs.

'Come on, come on!' said Twiddle, thinking it was the dog. He went out into the yard, where the kennel was. He couldn't see a thing, and he only knew he had come to the kennel when he bumped into it.

The cat came with him, rubbing against him.

'Go into your kennel, Tinker,' said Twiddle, thinking he was talking to the dog. Usually he heard Tinker's paws running into the kennel, but he didn't hear them tonight.

So he put out his hand, touched something warm, thought it was Tinker, and pushed him into the kennel. But it was the cat he had pushed. Mr Twiddle shut the kennel door, as he always did on cold nights. Now the dog was safe!

He went back into the house and bolted the door. He went upstairs. The dog lay on the couch, feeling very guilty and ashamed of himself, and wondering why Mr Twiddle hadn't fetched him. And when Mr and Mrs Twiddle were fast asleep in bed, the dog crept upstairs to them.

He lay down under the bed, not daring to wake Mr Twiddle. He soon fell asleep.

But Tinker always snored when he lay on his tummy with his head on his paws. And soon he began to make his little dog snores. 'Ur-r-r-r-r-r! Ur-r-r-r-r-r!'

Mrs Twiddle woke up with a jump and sat up in bed. She listened.

'Ur-r-r-r-r!' went Tinker, dreaming of bones and biscuits.

'Twiddle!' said Mrs Twiddle in a fright. 'There's somebody in the room!'

Twiddle woke up in astonishment. He sat up too. The noise awoke Tinker under the bed and he sat up as well, and stopped snoring. There was silence, whilst all three of them listened.

'There's nobody, wife,' said Twiddle crossly. 'What did the noise sound like?'

'Well, it really sounded rather like Tinker

snoring,' said Mrs Twiddle, puzzled. 'I suppose you *did* put the dog into his kennel, Twiddle?'

'Of course I did, *and* shut the door on him,' said Twiddle, settling down comfortably. 'Do go to sleep, wife.'

Mrs Twiddle lay down. Tinker lay down – but he made a big bump on the floor as he did so, and in a second Mrs Twiddle sat up again.

'There! Did you hear that? It was a bump!' she cried. But Twiddle was asleep, so, as she heard nothing more, Mrs Twiddle lay down. But soon Tinker began to snore again, and Mrs Twiddle woke Twiddle by shaking him hard.

'There's that noise again!' she said. 'Oh, do wake up, Twiddle! This is dreadful!'

Twiddle awoke. He felt angry. He lay and listened, but as Tinker was now awake again, he didn't snore. He was still feeling ashamed of himself because he hadn't gone to his kennel. He wanted to lick his master and mistress and say he was sorry.

Very quietly, he crept from under the bed, and sniffed till he found Twiddle's hand hanging down by the bed.

He licked it with his warm wet tongue. Twiddle was most surprised. He simply could *not* imagine what the wetness was. He didn't like it. He took his hand away.

Tinker was sad. He went to where Mrs Twiddle lay, on the other side of the bed. He put out his tongue and licked her nose.

'Ooooh!' squealed Mrs Twiddle in a fright, and sat up at once. 'Twiddle! Something licked me! I tell you something licked me!

On my nose, too!'

'Funny,' said Twiddle. 'Something licked me too.'

'If Tinker wasn't in his kennel, I'd think it was he who was here,' said Mrs Twiddle. 'Light the lamp!'

Twiddle lit it – and at once Tinker jumped up on the bed in delight. Mrs Twiddle gave another squeal. 'What is it, what is it? Oh – it's *you*, Tinker! Twiddle, you bad, untruthful man, you said you'd put him into his kennel. How dare you tell me such a story!'

'Well, I *did* put him there,' said Mr Twiddle, feeling as if he were in some kind of peculiar dream. 'But I'm not going out to put him there again, wife. If there's a Tinker in the kennel and a Tinker here too, we've got two dogs, that's all. Good night!'

He went to sleep at once. Mrs Twiddle pushed Tinker off the bed, and went to sleep as well, very puzzled and very angry.

Tinker kept jumping up on top of her, and she dreamed of elephants sitting on her all night long. Poor Mrs Twiddle!

And in the morning, when Twiddle went to see if there *was* another Tinker in the kennel, he let out a very angry cat, who spat at him and scratched him, furious at having been shut up all the night long, when she badly wanted to hunt mice!

'It serves you right, Twiddle,' said his wife, when she saw the scratch. 'If you don't know the difference between the dog and the cat at night, it's just about time you learnt!'

## Chapter 9
# Mr Twiddle and the Cat

Mr Twiddle had a cold. He sneezed and snuffled, and Mrs Twiddle was very sorry for him.

'You shall have a hot drink,' she said, 'and I will buy you some nice lozenges to suck. Now, just sit by the fire, Twiddle, and keep warm.'

Twiddle sat by the fire, and toasted his legs and knees. The cat came up and purred. It loved a warm fire as much as Mr Twiddle did.

Puss jumped up on to Mr Twiddle's knee, and dug a claw into his trousers to hold on by. Twiddle gave a yell!

'Ow! You tiresome cat! You've pricked me with your claw. Get down! I've enough to do with warming myself without having you on my knee too!'

He pushed the cat down. Puss waited a few minutes till Mr Twiddle shut his eyes and nodded – and then up jumped Puss again. Mr Twiddle got a shock. His pipe fell out of his mouth, and broke on the hearth.

He was very angry. 'Look at that!' he said to the cat. 'Now look what you've done, you careless, stupid animal! You deserve to be scolded.'

Now the more Twiddle lost his temper with the cat, the more Puss seemed to want to come to him. It was most annoying. First the cat lay down on his feet, and he had to shuffle it off. Then it jumped up on to the back of his chair and tried to lie round his neck. That made him very angry.

'Are you trying to be a scarf or something?' said Mr Twiddle to the cat. 'Get down! I don't want you on my feet and I don't want you round my neck. You are a real nuisance tonight. Do leave me alone.'

The cat disappeared. Mr Twiddle went to sleep. When he woke up he wanted to read the newspaper, so up he got to fetch it.

He didn't see the cat lying on the rug,

curled up in a ball. He trod on it, fell flat on his nose, and the cat leapt up and scratched his cheek. Dear me, what an upset there was! Mr Twiddle yelled, the cat yowled and spat, and Mrs Twiddle came running in to see what the matter was.

'Twiddle, how dare you be unkind to the cat!' she cried. Twiddle got up and glared at her.

'You just scold the cat, not me,' he said. 'It's she who is being unkind to *me*! She won't leave me alone!'

He felt for his glasses. They had fallen off his nose. Mr Twiddle went down on his hands and knees to find them. He put his hand under the sofa, but the cat was hiding there, and thought he was playing. So she patted his fingers, and made him jump.

'If that cat isn't under the sofa now!' said Mr Twiddle. 'Wife, I tell you she won't leave me alone! Take her away. I can't bear any more tonight.'

Mrs Twiddle took the cat into the scullery and shut the door on her. The cat jumped up on to the table, found Mr Twiddle's supper there, ready for cooking, and ate it all up. Dear me, how angry he was when he heard about it!

'I'm going to bed,' he said. 'I can't stand that cat any more. There's something strange about it tonight. It just won't leave me alone.'

'Don't be silly, Twiddle,' said his wife. She got up and went into the scullery. She filled a hot-water bottle and put a nice warm, furry cover on it. Then she went upstairs to put it into Twiddle's bed, whilst he went round the house and locked the doors.

Twiddle undressed. He grinned to himself when he thought of how he had shooed the cat out of the back door into the dark night. Now it wouldn't bother him any more. Ha ha! He wouldn't tell Mrs Twiddle. She would be cross if she knew the cat was out at night.

He threw back the sheets and jumped into bed. He put his feet down – and good gracious me, whatever was that in the bed? Twiddle gave a loud yell, jumped out again, and glared fearfully at the lump in the bed.

'That cat again!' he said. 'How did it get there? No sooner did I put my feet down than I felt it, all warm and furry. It's a magic cat tonight. What am I to do? I simply don't dare to get into bed. I shan't tell Mrs Twiddle. She will only laugh at me.'

Mrs Twiddle was sleeping in the spare-room bed that night, because she didn't want to catch Twiddle's cold. Her light was out. Twiddle stood in his bedroom and shivered.

'Fancy that tiresome cat thinking it would sleep in my bed!' he said to himself. 'Whatever next? And I shooed it out of the back door too! Well, I shall put on my dressing-gown and spend the night in my chair in front of the kitchen fire. If that cat thinks it's going to bite my toes all night, it's mistaken!'

Poor Twiddle! He went downstairs to sit by the fire. He was almost asleep when Mrs Twiddle appeared, looking most surprised.

'Twiddle! Whatever are you doing? I looked in your room to see if you were all right, and you weren't there!'

'I couldn't get into bed,' said Twiddle sulkily. 'That cat was there.'

'Don't be silly, Twiddle. She never goes upstairs,' said Mrs Twiddle.

'I'm not silly,' said Twiddle. 'I tell you, that cat is lying in my bed, and I'm not going to sleep with it.'

Just then there came a mewing outside the back door, and something scratched and scraped at the door.

'But *that's* the cat!' cried Mrs Twiddle in surprise. 'I'd know her mew anywhere! However is it that she's outside, poor darling!'

'That's not the cat,' said Twiddle. 'I tell you, she's upstairs in my bed, as warm as a pie.'

Mrs Twiddle opened the back door – and in bounded the cat, purring with delight. She jumped straight on to Twiddle's knee. He gave a yell.

'Get off! Wife, there must be two cats then. I tell you one is asleep in my bed.'

'Well, we'll come and see,' said Mrs Twiddle, thinking that Twiddle must be quite mad. They went upstairs, and Mrs Twiddle threw back the covers. In the middle of the bed was the hot-water bottle she had put there, warm and cosy in its furry cover!

'You thought your hot-water bottle was the c-c-c-cat!' cried Mrs Twiddle, beginning to laugh and laugh. 'And you went downstairs in a rage, and left your lovely hot bottle to sleep in the bed by itself! Oh, Twiddle! Oh, Twiddle, you'll make me die of laughing one of these days!'

She laughed till she cried. Twiddle was angry and ashamed. He got into bed, put his feet on the hot bottle, and covered himself up.

'I'll have no more to do with that cat from now on,' he said. But, dear me, as soon as he was asleep, Puss jumped up on his bed and slept peacefully on Twiddle's feet all night long. Wouldn't Twiddle have been cross if he'd known!

## Chapter 10
# Mr Twiddle and the Dog

Once Mrs Twiddle looked after a friend's dog for a week. It was a nice little dog, called Scamp. It was most obedient, always wiped its paws on the mat when it came indoors, and said 'Wuff-wuff' for its food.

'Really, I'm quite sorry to part with the dog,' said Mrs Twiddle, patting it. 'Twiddle, will you take it back for me, please? My friend, Mrs Gubbins, would like to have it this morning.'

'Certainly, my dear, certainly!' said Mr Twiddle. 'Shall I go now? There's a bus I can catch in about ten minutes' time.'

'Yes – get your hat and go along,' said Mrs Twiddle. She gave the dog a biscuit, brushed his coat well, and fastened the lead to his collar.

'Dear, dear!' she said, feeling the collar. 'You must have grown fatter this week, Scamp. Your collar is too tight for your neck. I'll loosen it!'

She undid the collar and slipped the buckle along to another hole. The dog liked its collar loose. It knew it could slip it off then! It licked Mrs Twiddle's hands.

'Dear little thing,' said Mrs Twiddle. 'Now, Twiddle, hurry along or you'll miss that bus.'

Twiddle looked for his hat, put it on, and then, looking at his watch, he found that he only had about five minutes. He took hold of the lead and shot off down the garden path, with the dog trotting after him. When he got to the gate Mr Twiddle found that he had forgotten to put his glasses on. He had cleaned them and left them on the table. Bother!

'Well, never mind, I shan't really need them,' said Mr Twiddle, hurrying along. 'I shall miss the bus if I don't walk fast.'

Now very soon the dog met a friend. This friend was a beautiful little Pekinese, and Scamp thought she was marvellous. The

Pekinese wagged her feathery tail and Scamp wagged his.

'Stop a minute and talk to me,' said the Pekinese. So Scamp did a kind of double wriggle, and slipped his head neatly out of his loose collar. He wagged his tail at the Pekinese, and joyfully licked her nose. He was ready for a jolly good game!

The Pekinese looked after Mr Twiddle in astonishment. 'Does he mind going without you?' she asked.

'I haven't asked him,' said Scamp. 'I say, doesn't my collar look funny running along the road without me on the end of the lead! What will Twiddle say when he sees it?'

With a bound Scamp ran round the corner and began to have a fine game with his little friend. Mr Twiddle didn't even see him go. He trotted along down the street, pulling the lead and empty collar behind him, whistling a little tune, and keeping a sharp lookout for the bus at the corner.

He met his friend, Mr Jinks, who stared in astonishment at the sight of Twiddle hurrying along pulling a collar behind him.

'Where are you going?' he called.

'Just taking this dear little dog back to its

owner,' said Twiddle, beaming. 'Isn't it a good little soul, trotting along behind me so happily?'

Mr Jinks thought that Mr Twiddle must be a little mad that morning. But there wasn't any time to say so because Twiddle hurried on so quickly. Mr Jinks stared at the collar

running along behind Mr Twiddle, and
began to laugh.

Mr Twiddle got to the corner just at the
same moment as the bus did. He jumped up,
and pulled the lead and collar behind him.

'Now just go under the seat and lie down
quietly,' said Mr Twiddle, peering round for
Scamp. He couldn't see him, so he thought
he must have gone under the seat already.

'Good dog,' he said to the empty collar
there. 'Very good dog! Conductor, I want a
ticket for myself, and a ticket for my dog.'

'What dog?' asked the conductor in
amazement.

'The dog with me, of course,' said Mr
Twiddle. 'Really, some people do ask silly
questions. Don't you know a dog when you
see one? Perhaps you thought I had a cat or
a canary on my lead.'

The conductor looked offended. He
thought that if Mr Twiddle really wanted to
buy a ticket for a dog that wasn't there, he
might as well let him. So he gave him a ticket
and a dog's ticket as well.

A very big lady got in with a small dog
under her arm. She tried to sit down beside
Mr Twiddle.

'Madam, I have a dog under my seat,' said Mr Twiddle. 'Perhaps it would be better if you took the seat over there. Our two dogs might fight.'

The big lady looked under the seat and saw no dog at all. Only an empty collar. She thought it was a trick to make her take another seat and leave Mr Twiddle comfortably alone in his.

So she sat down opposite to him and glared at him with large black eyes. Mr Twiddle felt most uncomfortable.

'I suppose you think you are very clever,' said the big lady in a freezing sort of voice.

Mr Twiddle was astonished. He had never thought himself clever, to begin with – and he couldn't imagine why the big lady should think he did. He felt more and more uncomfortable as he sat under the glare of the lady's big black eyes, and he bent down and spoke to Scamp, whom he still thought was lying quietly under the seat.

It was dark under the seat, and Mr Twiddle hadn't got his glasses, so he couldn't see a thing. He spoke in a quiet voice.

'Good dog, Scamp. Very good dog. Lie down quietly now.'

Not a sound came from under the seat, which wasn't at all surprising.

'You do think you're funny, don't you?' said the big lady in a scornful sort of voice.

'Well, Madam, no, I can't say that I have ever thought myself funny,' said Twiddle. He got up to go, because he couldn't bear to think what the strange big lady would say next. 'Come on, Scamp!' he said. 'Come on.'

'Mind he doesn't bite you!' called the big lady after him. Twiddle thought that was a silly remark. He jumped off the bus, and with his nose well up in the air he hurried along.

'Hie! Your dog's gone to chase a cat!' a boy shouted after him.

'Silly child!' thought Twiddle, pulling the lead behind him. 'Thinks he'll make me look behind and see if Scamp really has gone chasing cats. Well, I won't!'

'Hie! Your dog's lost!' yelled another boy.

'Dear me, I wonder why children are so stupid this morning,' thought poor Twiddle. 'Ah – here is Mrs Gubbins's house!'

He went up the path and knocked at the door. Mrs Gubbins opened it.

'Oh, do come in,' she said. 'I wondered if you'd bring back my darling Scamp today!'

'Then you wondered right,' said Twiddle happily, pulling the collar behind him in the hall. 'I've brought him – and he's been as good as gold all the time!'

He looked round to see Scamp, but the hall was dark, and he could see nothing. 'He must have gone under the chest there!' he said. 'Scamp! Scamp!'

'But he didn't come in with you,' said Mrs Gubbins, puzzled. 'At least, *I* never saw him!'

'He was just at my heels,' said Mr Twiddle.

'I had him on the lead.'

He pulled at the lead – and the empty collar slid over the floor to Mr Twiddle's foot. Mr Twiddle bent down to pat the dog that wasn't there. His hand found the empty collar and he picked it up and blinked at it.

'Good gracious!' he said. 'He's slipped his collar, the rascal. Well, I'm sure he's under the chest, Mrs Gubbins. You call him and see. I must go now or I'll miss the bus back. Goodbye, Scamp, dear little chap! Goodbye!'

He trotted off down the path again to the bus, whilst Mrs Gubbins looked all about for a dog she couldn't find. Twiddle caught the bus and was soon trotting home down the street.

'Well!' cried Mrs Twiddle, opening the door to him, 'and where have *you* been all this time? Didn't I tell you to take Scamp back to Mrs Gubbins for me?'

'Well, my dear, I did,' said Twiddle, in surprise. 'He was as good as gold all the way, and I left him safely under the chest in the hall at Mrs Gubbins's.'

'Oh – and I suppose he caught the bus back, and arrived home before you did,' said Mrs Twiddle, in a rage. 'Scamp! Come here!'

And to poor Twiddle's enormous astonishment Scamp came rushing out of the kitchen, put his front paws on Twiddle's middle, and tried to reach up and lick him.

'But I've just taken you to your mistress!' cried Twiddle, sitting down in alarm. 'Wife, there must be two Scamps. There really must.'

'Well, it's a good thing there's not two Twiddles!' said Mrs Twiddle with a snort. 'Now *I* shall have to take Scamp home myself – and without a collar and lead too. Really, Twiddle!'

She looked so fierce that poor Twiddle ran out to the garden shed and sat there the rest of the day. And he still cannot think how it was that he took Scamp home – and yet found him waiting for him when he came back!'

### Chapter 11
# Mr Twiddle's Spectacles

'Have you seen my spectacles, Mrs Twiddle?' asked Mr Twiddle, looking all round for them.

'Oh, dear! Have you lost them *again*?' sighed Mrs Twiddle. 'I'm getting so tired of it, Twiddle. Twenty times a day you say the same thing to me – "Have you seen my spectacles?" Why don't you keep them in the same place, whenever you take them off, then you would know where they were.'

'That's a good idea,' said Mr Twiddle, blinking all round the room to see if he could find them. 'But what is a safe place? Wherever I put them, they seem to disappear at once.'

'Oh no they don't,' said Mrs Twiddle. 'You

just put them down anywhere and forget them – then you look for them in the wrong place and say they've gone. Why, I found them inside the teapot yesterday, Twiddle. Whatever made you put them there?'

'Dear me, were they really there?' said Twiddle. 'Well, I wonder if they are there now.'

But they weren't. Twiddle looked round everywhere, but his glasses really did seem to have vanished this time.

'When did you last take them off?' asked Mrs Twiddle, knitting away hard.

'Let me see now – oh yes, I took them off in the bathroom when I went to wash my face,' said Mr Twiddle. 'Yes, I distinctly remember doing that.'

'Well, you have probably put your spectacles in the bath then, if I know anything about you,' said Mrs Twiddle. 'You had better go and look.'

Mr Twiddle went – and he came back looking rather foolish. He had his glasses on his nose.

'You were quite right, my dear,' he said to Mrs Twiddle. 'I *had* put them into the bath. I suppose I thought they would be safe there whilst I washed. And, of course, I left them there by mistake.'

'Now listen to me, Twiddle,' said Mrs Twiddle. 'You just think of some really good place to put your glasses whenever you take them off – and *always* put them there – and then you will never, never have to look for them. You will always know exactly where they are.'

'That *is* a good idea, Wife,' said Twiddle, pleased. 'Now where would be a good place? On top of the clock, do you think?'

'And do you think you could easily get them off the clock if you are out to tea?' said Mrs Twiddle. 'Or suppose you are at the bottom of the garden – will you like coming all the way into the house to fetch them? No – you won't. Now be sensible, Twiddle, and think of some safe place that is easy to get at wherever you are.'

Mrs Twiddle heard the back door bell and she got up to answer it. Twiddle stood and thought about his glasses. Where would be the best place to keep them? He thought and thought – and then he smiled.

'*I* know a good place!' he said. 'I'll put them into their brown leather case – and slip the case into one of my socks! Then whenever I want my glasses, all I shall have to do will be to bend down and slip the case out of my sock. Ah, that *is* a good place, to be sure!'

He put his glasses into their case, bent down and pulled up his trouser leg – and slipped the fat brown case into the top of his sock. The suspender kept it tight. His glasses would be quite safe there. Really, that was a very clever idea.

Mrs Twiddle called to him. 'Twiddle! The fish hasn't come yet! I must go out and get it. I shan't be long.'

'Very well, dear,' called back Mr Twiddle. 'I'll answer the bells whilst you are gone.' Mrs Twiddle went out. Mr Twiddle made up the kitchen fire. He shooed the cat away from the larder. He cleaned his shoes slowly till they shone like black polished wood. And then he felt that he really did deserve a sitdown!

So down he sat in his armchair. He took up the paper and began to read – but, dear me, he couldn't see to read without his glasses! So he looked on the table for them.

They were not there, of course. They were in his left sock. But dear old Twiddle had forgotten all about that. He got up and looked in his chair seat. Sometimes he left his glasses there. But no, they were not there this time.

'Dear, dear! Gone again!' said Mr Twiddle, really cross. 'Now how am I to read without my glasses?'

He hunted all round the kitchen. He hunted all over the bedroom. He hunted everywhere – except in his left sock! Then he wondered what Mrs Twiddle would say if she came home and found him hunting for his glasses again.

'I am sure I must have dropped them out-of-doors somewhere,' said Twiddle. 'I've looked simply everywhere *in*doors. Yes – I must have dropped them in the road. Dear, dear – what a sad thing! I must put a notice in the paper to say I will give a reward to anyone finding them.'

Mrs Twiddle came back at that minute and Twiddle called to her, 'I'm just going out for a minute, dear. I won't be long.'

So out he went to the newspaper office. The man there said yes, he could put a notice into the paper about Mr Twiddle's glasses. He pushed a sheet of notepaper over to him.

'Just write down what you want us to put into the paper,' he said. 'What sort of glasses they are, and so on.'

Mr Twiddle took the paper and a pen. He stood and thought. Yes – he knew what to say. He would say 'LOST – a nice pair of tortoiseshell glasses. Finder will be given one pound fifty.'

He began to write the notice down – but he couldn't very well see without his glasses. He fumbled about for them in his pocket. Then he beamed. Of course – they were in his sock. He bent down, turned up his trouser leg, and took out his spectacle case from his sock.

He put the case on the table and opened it. He took out his spectacles and put them on his nose. Then he noticed that the man was staring at him very hard.

'Staring is rude,' said Mr Twiddle. 'Is anything wrong with me?'

'No,' said the man, and he giggled.

'What's the joke?' asked Mr Twiddle crossly. 'Am *I* the joke?'

'Well – yes, in a way,' said the man. 'Write out the notice, please, sir.'

Grumbling away to himself, Mr Twiddle wrote out his notice. Then he gave it to the man, who read it and chuckled. He looked at Mr Twiddle and held out his hand.

'One pound fifty, please, sir,' he said. 'I've found your glasses for you.'

'No, really!' cried Twiddle, excited. 'Where did you find them? Do tell me!'

'Here they are,' said the man, and he neatly took them off Twiddle's nose, put them into his case, and handed them to Twiddle. 'One pound fifty, reward, please.'

'B-b-b-b-b-but,' stammered Twiddle. 'B-b-but – how did they get there?'

'Well, you took them out of your sock and put them on your nose yourself,' said the man, giggling. 'Now, Mr Twiddle, pay up. It would cost you two pounds to put that notice into the paper – but it will only cost you one pound fifty reward. I did find them, didn't I – on your nose!'

Mr Twiddle paid one pound fifty in disgust. How could he be so silly as to offer a reward to anyone finding his glasses when they were on his nose all the time!

He went home and told Mrs Twiddle all about it. 'And where are your glasses now?' asked Mrs Twiddle, seeing that they were not on his nose.

'I expect they are in my sock,' said Mr Twiddle, and he bent down to look. But, you know, they were *not* there! Mr Twiddle scratched his head and frowned.

'Oh dear!' he said. 'Oh dear – I must have left them on the table at the paper office. Yes – that man must have got them there. Dear, dear, dear – I hope I shan't have to pay him another one pound fifty  for finding them!'

Off he went to get them. Really, it's a wonder he ever has them at all, isn't it!

## Chapter 12
# Mr Twiddle Goes Out at Night

One night Mr and Mrs Twiddle were asked to go to Mr Fankle's birthday party.

'Mr Fankle doesn't get home till seven o'clock,' said Mrs Fankle, 'so it will have to be a supper party. Can you come?'

'We'd love to,' said Mrs Twiddle. 'Only it is so dreadfully dark at night now. Still, we have our torches, and we'll come along, Mrs Fankle. Thank you for the invitation.'

'I know!' cried Mrs Fankle suddenly. '*You* come along to tea with me in the afternoon, Mrs Twiddle, and help me to get the supper things ready. Then you won't need to come here in the dark. Twiddle can come along by himself quite easily, can't he?'

'Oh yes,' said Mrs Twiddle. 'I'll leave all his things ready for him, and he can dress himself and come along at eight o'clock.'

So, on the day of Mr Fankle's party, Mrs Twiddle called to Mr Twiddle.

'Twiddle! I am leaving all your things ready for you here!' she cried. 'There is your evening cloak – your top hat – your best white handkerchief – your stick – and a parcel in which I've put your present for Mr Fankle.'

'Yes, dear,' said Mr Twiddle, not really paying much attention. 'Yes, dear. I'll remember, dear.'

Now Mrs Twiddle was calling from his bedroom, where she had laid out all the things for Mr Twiddle. But, Twiddle thought she was calling from the kitchen, and so, that night, when he wanted to go to the party, he walked out to the kitchen to get ready.

There was nobody there. Mr Twiddle did not dare to light a lamp, because Mrs Twiddle had not drawn the curtains before she had left that afternoon, and Mr Twiddle knew that his wife would not have a light on unless the window was covered.

So he began to feel about for his things. Of course they were not there – they were up in his bedroom; but Mr Twiddle didn't think of that. He wandered round the dark kitchen, feeling here and there for his things – but, dear me! he couldn't seem to find them at all!

'Where *has* Mrs Twiddle put them?' he said crossly. 'Really, she's a very silly woman. Why didn't she put them on the table, where I could easily get them? And why didn't she draw the curtains before she went so that I could light a lamp and see what I am doing?'

Mr Twiddle didn't think of drawing the curtains himself. He just went on looking and looking. He brushed against the table, and the cloth fell on the floor. When Mr Twiddle went walking round that side of the table again, he stumbled over the cloth.

'Ah! There's my cloak!' he said, and bent to pick it up. 'Fancy Mrs Twiddle putting it on the floor. Silly woman!'

He tried his best to put the tablecloth on like a cloak, but he couldn't. So he just wrapped it somehow round himself, and then felt about for his hat.

'That may be on the floor too,' said Mr

Twiddle. 'If Mrs Twiddle put my cloak on the floor, I expect she will have put my hat there too. Dear, dear, dear!'

So he felt round the floor, and came to the waste-paper basket. It was round and tall, and felt to Mr Twiddle just like his hat. He picked it up and put it on. Luckily it was empty.

'Seems a bit tight for me,' said Mr Twiddle, puzzled. 'My head must have grown! Well, well! never mind, that's my hat found. Now for my white handkerchief.'

He found a duster on the dresser, and stuffed that into his pocket, leaving a little bit of yellow hanging out. Then he hunted for his stick.

He found the poker, though he thought it felt rather heavier than usual for a stick. However, he tucked it under his arm, and was just about to go when he remembered the parcel for Mr Fankle's birthday.

'Gracious! I nearly forgot it!' he said, and began to hunt around again for a parcel. He soon found one, though he didn't know it was only Mrs Twiddle's old boots wrapped up to give away to the rag and bone man. He put it under his arm and set off, banging the door behind him.

He wore the bright red kitchen tablecloth round his shoulders, the waste-paper basket for a hat; he had a yellow duster in his pocket instead of a handkerchief, and he carried the kitchen poker for his stick. Really, Mr Twiddle!

He knocked at Mr Fankle's door. He was

late, and everyone else had arrived.

'That must be Mr Twiddle?' cried Mrs Fankle, and she ran to the door to open it, followed by all the others. Twiddle stepped inside. The door shut, and Mrs Fankle switched on the light.

And then there was an astonished silence, as everyone looked at Mr Twiddle. *How* peculiar he looked!

'Well, what's the matter?' asked Mr Twiddle, puzzled.

'Er – have you come in fancy dress?' asked Mr Fankle, trying not to laugh.

'Of course not,' said Mr Twiddle crossly. And then he stared at the waste-paper basket he had taken off his head. He looked at the red kitchen cloth – and the poker. He went very red.

'Twiddle!' cried Mrs Twiddle. 'Whatever have you dressed yourself up like that for? You *do* look silly!'

'It was a mistake,' said Twiddle, putting down the basket, and taking off the red cloth. He stood the poker in the umbrella stand, and tried to look merry and bright. He felt hot and bothered, so he took out his handkerchief to mop his head – and pulled out the yellow kitchen duster!

'Twiddle!' squealed Mrs Twiddle. 'My duster! What did you take that for?'

Twiddle threw the duster down in a temper. Then he gave the parcel to Mr Fankle.

'Many happy returns of the day,' he said. 'Here is a little present for you.'

'Oh, thank you,' said Mr Fankle, and undid the parcel. Out fell Mrs Twiddle's holey old boots!

'Well, really, what a funny present!' said Mr Fankle, puzzled. Mrs Twiddle began to laugh.

'Oh, he's brought the wrong parcel!' she said. 'I know what he's done, the silly man! He looked for his things in the dark kitchen instead of upstairs in the bedroom where there is a light and where I had put out all his clothes, *and* the right parcel! Oh, Twiddle! Oh, Twiddle! I shall die of laughing, I know I shall!'

And she began to laugh and laugh and laugh. Everyone else laughed too – really, what *would* old Twiddle do next? Who would have thought anyone would have worn a waste-paper basket for a hat and the kitchen tablecloth for a cloak!

Twiddle stood there looking sulky and red – and then *he* suddenly began to laugh too. You should have heard him – ha, ha, ha! ho, ho, ho! he, he, he!

'Yes,' he said, wiping his eyes, 'I'm a silly fellow – but anyway, I've given you a good joke for your birthday, Mr Fankle!' And he certainly had!

## Chapter 13
## *Mr Twiddle Is a Funny Fellow*

One morning Mrs Twiddle wanted to make some buns and she found that she had no eggs.

'Twiddle!' she cried. 'Where are you? Oh, there you are, asleep in a deck chair in the sun as usual! Get up, lazybones, and go and do a little shopping for me.'

'I wasn't asleep, my dear – I only just shut my eyes because the sun was rather bright,' said Mr Twiddle, getting up at once.

'Well, if you were awake, it's funny you should snore,' said Mrs Twiddle. 'Now, Twiddle, take my basket – it's over there. And go to the grocer's, and ask for three eggs, a small bag of flour, and a pound of currants. Hurry now, because my oven is getting nice and hot for the buns.'

Twiddle took the basket and hurried. He ran down the road to the grocer's. He asked for a bag of flour, which the grocer gave him. A pound of currants, and he got those too. But when he asked for three eggs, the grocer shook his head.

'Sorry, sir,' he said, 'but I've no eggs today. I may have some tomorrow.'

'But Mrs Twiddle will be very cross with me if I go home without eggs,' said Twiddle in dismay. 'You see she wants to make buns, and her oven is getting hot.'

'That's a pity,' said the grocer. 'Well, look,

Mr Twiddle, sir – take some egg powder instead. It will do quite well in place of eggs.'

'All right, I will,' said Twiddle. The grocer shook some yellow egg powder into a paper, twisted it up, and gave it to Twiddle. He paid the bill, put the things into his basket, and set out again for home.

He bought some tobacco for himself, and a paper, and then stood for a moment at the gate of a field. It was full of golden buttercups, and looked very lovely.

'I think I will walk home through the fields,' said Mr Twiddle to himself. 'It will do me good. And those buttercups are beautiful to see.'

So off he went through the buttercup fields. His legs brushed against hundreds of golden buttercup heads, and they shook their yellow pollen against his trousers. And when dear old Twiddle came out into the road again he found that his trouser legs were covered with yellow powder!

'Goodness gracious! Look at that! What can it be? It's something that has fallen out of the bottom of my basket!' said Twiddle in dismay. He stared at his basket, and remembered what he had in it.

'Yes – it must be the egg powder! It was bright yellow, I remember. The grocer must have twisted up the packet so loosely that all the powder has dribbled out of it, through the bottom of my basket and down my trouser legs,' said Twiddle. He felt rather clever to have thought all this out.

He scratched his head and thought hard again.

'I must go back and get some more. It's no good going home with an empty packet, and Mrs Twiddle asking for eggs,' he said to himself.

So back he went to the grocer's. 'I'm sorry,' said Mr Twiddle, 'but all the egg powder has fallen out of the packet down my trousers. Look at it! I must have some more.'

'You must have put it rather carelessly into your basket,' said the grocer. He brushed all the yellow powder from Twiddle's trousers and gave him another packet, very firmly twisted up indeed. Twiddle carefully poked it down into his basket and set off again. He thought he would have time to walk through the fields again. It had been so very pleasant last time.

'The buttercups are like a big golden carpet spread out for a king to tread upon,' said Twiddle to himself, and he pretended that he was the king, and walked on very haughtily, his head in the air.

And, of course, when he came out into the road again, what did he see but yellow powder all over his trouser legs once more!

'Well, really, this is very vexing!' said Twiddle, annoyed. 'The second lot of egg powder has shaken out of the basket too! That grocer *does* pack his things carelessly.'

So back he ran to the grocer's again, feeling hot and out of breath. He banged his basket down on the floor. 'Look at my trouser legs again!' he cried. 'That egg powder of yours has shaken loose from the package once more! I've lost it all! Get me some more, please, and put it into a tight-lidded box this time!'

The grocer was busy and cross. He told his boy to give the powder to Twiddle in a box with a very tight-fitting lid.

The boy put it into the basket, and Twiddle marched off for the third time. He looked at his watch and decided that he hadn't time to go through the fields again. He had better run all the way down the road!

So he set off, and arrived home very hot and panting indeed.

'What a long time you've been!' cried Mrs Twiddle. 'Here I've been waiting and waiting for those things, and my oven's so hot now that it would roast a large turkey!'

Twiddle put the basket on the table and wiped his forehead. 'Now I'll just tell you what's happened,' he began. 'It was most annoying . . .'

'Oh, I haven't time to hear your excuses!' cried Mrs Twiddle. 'Did you bring the eggs?'

'No,' said Twiddle. 'There are no eggs today. So I brought egg powder instead. And just let me tell you about that – the grocer was very foolish and . . .'

'Go into the garden, Twiddle!' cried Mrs Twiddle, who was anxious to get on with her cake-making. 'I'll listen to you after I've done my baking!'

Twiddle was cross. He went into the garden and sank into his deck chair with his pipe and paper. But he was so tired that he fell fast asleep.

But not for long! Out came Mrs Twiddle, carrying two packets and a box, and looking very puzzled indeed.

'Twiddle! Twiddle!' she cried. 'You must really be quite mad! You have brought back two packets of egg powder and a boxful too! I shan't want so much. It is most extravagant of you!'

Twiddle woke with a jump. He stared at the two packets and the box. They were all quite full of egg powder, fine and yellow. He stared at the yellow powder on his trousers, and he thought he must be dreaming.

'It's all right,' he told his wife. 'I'm just dreaming this. I couldn't spill two packets of egg powder down my trousers, and still bring two full packets home and a box too. So I must be dreaming. Don't worry about it. I shall wake up in a minute, and then you will see that the two packets are empty, not full.'

'Twiddle! Don't be so silly!' cried Mrs Twiddle, most annoyed. 'You may be asleep and dreaming, but I most certainly am not! I tell you there are three lots of egg powder, and I INSIST on you telling me why you bought three instead of one.'

Well, of course, that was just what poor old Twiddle couldn't do. He stared at the egg powder in the packets, and he stared at the powder on his trouser legs, and he never once thought it was buttercup pollen. So how could he explain anything to Mrs Twiddle?

She was cross. He was upset. And the buns burnt in the hot oven. So altogether it was a most unlucky day, and only the buttercups that nodded their heads in the summer breeze knew the meaning of the puzzle!

## Chapter 14
# Mr Twiddle Tries to Help

Once Mrs Twiddle twisted her ankle and couldn't get about as usual to do her work. Mr Twiddle was very sorry for her.

'Now, my dear, you just sit down and let me run about for you!' he said. 'I've got a pair of legs, haven't I? Well, I can do everything just as well as you!'

'You want brains as well as legs, dear Twiddle,' said Mrs Twiddle, sitting down with a sigh. 'Oh, my poor ankle! Well well – you must do a little to help me, Twiddle, that's quite certain.'

Twiddle worked quite well for a while. He wrote out the list for the washing. He dusted the drawing-room. He fed the cat. Then he felt really tired and he sat down to have a rest.

117

Mrs Twiddle called to him. 'Twiddle! Twiddle! Where have you got to? There's somebody at the back door. And did you put the pudding in the oven as I told you to?'

Twiddle was half asleep. He got up at once, and, rubbing his eyes, he went to the back door. A boy was there with a clock.

'Your clock's mended, sir,' said the boy, and gave Mr Twiddle his lovely drawing-room clock. Mr Twiddle was pleased. He had missed the clock, because it struck the half-hours and chimed the hours. It was a nice clock.

'It's the clock come back,' he said to Mrs Twiddle. 'I must just put it on the drawing-room mantelpiece.'

'Oh, Twiddle, I do wish you'd put the rice pudding into the oven first,' said Mrs Twiddle. 'I keep asking you to. It won't be ready by dinner time if you don't. Do do as you are told, if you really want to help me!'

'All right, all right, my dear,' said Twiddle, still half asleep. And whatever *do* you think he did?

Why, he put the drawing-room clock into the oven and then picked up the rice pudding in its enamel dish and put it carefully on the drawing-room mantelpiece!

He just wasn't thinking what he was doing, of course. He shut the oven door on the clock and then went to see what else he could do.

Mrs Twiddle hadn't noticed anything. She was knitting hard. The cat gave a mew when it saw the pudding in the middle of the drawing-room mantelpiece, but nobody took any notice of the mew. So the cat settled down and went to sleep.

After a bit the clock in the oven struck the half-hour. Mrs Twiddle looked up.

'Why, Twiddle,' she said, 'that clock is somewhere in the kitchen! I distinctly heard it strike.'

'How can it strike in the kitchen when I put it in the drawing-room?' asked Twiddle, feeling cross. 'You do say surprising things, Wife.'

'Well, I suppose I was mistaken,' said Mrs Twiddle, knitting again.

Now, at twelve o'clock, the clock not only struck twelve times, but chimed too!

Ding, dong, ding, dong! it went; ding, dong, ding, dong!

'Twiddle! That clock is certainly in the kitchen!' said Mrs Twiddle.

Well, Twiddle had heard it strike and chime as well, and he too felt sure it was in the kitchen. So he looked round, but he couldn't see it anywhere, of course. This wasn't surprising, as it was still in the oven.

'I can't understand it, Wife,' said Twiddle, scratching his head. 'I distinctly remember taking it into the drawing-room.'

'Twiddle, just look and see if the milk pudding is getting on all right,' said Mrs Twiddle. 'It should be doing nicely now.'

Twiddle opened the oven door – and inside was the drawing-room clock, looking out at him with a very surprised face, because it was slowly cooking and didn't like it at all!

'*Twiddle!* You surely didn't put the clock to cook in the oven!' cried Mrs Twiddle. 'Oh,

Twiddle – and we've just had it mended. Oh, I'm sure it will have done it no good to cook like that. You foolish man! Take it out at once!'

So Twiddle, looking very foolish, took it out and set it on the shelf to cool. It made a very peculiar noise and then stopped ticking.

'It's stopped!' said Mrs Twiddle. 'Now it will have to go and be mended again – and it's only just come back! Really, Twiddle! And what about the pudding? Did you look in the oven and see how that is doing?'

Twiddle looked – but of course the pudding wasn't there. It was most extraordinary. 'I know I *put* it there!' said Twiddle. 'I feel sure I did. But it's vanished.'

Just then there came a knock at the front door. 'There's Mrs Harris,' said Mrs Twiddle. 'Show her into the drawing-room, please, Twiddle, and say I will come in half a minute. I must just put my shoe on.'

Twiddle went to the front door and showed Mrs Harris into the drawing-room. He said that Mrs Twiddle would only be a minute. And it wasn't long before his wife was hobbling into the drawing-room with a stick.

'Good morning, Mrs Twiddle,' said Mrs Harris. 'Did you know that your cat was eating an uncooked rice pudding in the middle of the mantelpiece? I just wondered if that was the usual place to give her her dinner.'

Mrs Twiddle looked at the mantelpiece in horror – and sure enough there was Puss lapping up the milk and the rice for all she was worth, enjoying such an unusual treat!

'Shoo, Puss, shoo!' cried Mrs Twiddle, clapping her hands at once. The cat leapt off and upset the dish. The milk dripped into the fender and the dish fell with a clatter.

'Twiddle! Twiddle! You put the pudding on the mantelpiece instead of the clock, and you put the clock in the oven instead of the pudding!' cried Mrs Twiddle. 'Oh, it's much quicker to do things myself! What a stupid, foolish man you are, to be sure!'

And poor Twiddle thought the same as he fetched a cloth to mop up the milky mess. 'I've got to pay to mend the clock again,' he thought sadly. 'And I've spoilt the pudding. But never mind about that! I never *did* like rice puddings!'

Whatever will he do next? I really can't think!

# Don't Be Silly,
# Mr Twiddle!

# Don't Be Silly,
# Mr Twiddle!

Enid Blyton

*Illustrations by Stephen Dell*

BLOOMSBURY
CHILDREN'S
BOOKS

# Contents

## Chapter 1

# *Don't be Silly, Mr Twiddle*

Once Mrs Twiddle was in bed with a bad cold.

Mr Twiddle was very sorry, and he said he would do what he could to help. But Mrs Twiddle thought to herself that she wasn't sure if Twiddle's help would be much use.

'You tell Mrs Minny, the woman who comes to do the washing today, to come up and see me,' said Mrs Twiddle, sneezing into her handkerchief. 'She can do everything for me, and cook your dinner, and do a bit of washing as well.'

So Mrs Minny went up to see Mrs Twiddle, and the two of them planned out the day's work.

'If you can scrub the kitchen floor, and

cook a bit of dinner, and wash out that dirty sheet over there and sponge that oily mark out of Mr Twiddle's coat, and see that the cat has her dinner, I think we'd be all right,' said Mrs Twiddle. 'Could you do that, do you think?'

'Oh, yes, easily,' said kind Mrs Minny. 'Mr Twiddle doesn't need to do a thing.'

They sent Mr Twiddle out to the chemist's so that he would be out of the way, because very often when he wanted to be helpful, he wasn't at all. Then Mrs Minny set to work to peel potatoes and make a pie, and scrub the kitchen floor and do a bit of washing.

She hung the washed sheet out in the garden and she pegged up Mr Twiddle's sponged coat on the line, too, so that they would both dry in the wind. She took up Mrs Twiddle's dinner on a tray and she gave Mr Twiddle his as well. Then she washed up and said goodbye.

'Everything's done,' she said, 'and I've left a cold supper in the larder. If Mr Twiddle will just bring in the coat and the sheet off the line, when they're dry, that's all there is to do.'

'Thank you, Mrs Minny,' said Mrs Twiddle. I'm very grateful. I'll tell Mr Twiddle.'

Well, after Mrs Minny had gone, Mrs Twiddle happened to look out of the window, and it was pouring with rain. The drops splashed down, and Mrs Twiddle remembered the sheet and the coat hanging out on the line in the garden. She called loudly to Twiddle.

'Twiddle! Twiddle! Go out and bring in the sheet and the coat out of the wet.'

Twiddle was asleep. He awoke with a jump and got up out of his armchair. 'Bring in the sheep and goat?' he said, sleepily. 'What sheep and goat, dear?'

Mrs Twiddle called downstairs again, impatiently. 'It's raining, Twiddle, that's why I want the sheet and the coat brought indoors. Go and bring them in.'

Well, Twiddle still thought Mrs Twiddle said 'Sheep' and 'Goat', and he was rather surprised. So he called up again. 'Do you really mean the sheep and the goat?'

Mrs Twiddle thought he said 'the sheet and the coat,' and answered crossly.

'Are you *trying* to be stupid, Twiddle? Is there anything funny about bringing in a sheet and a coat out of the rain? I don't want them to get wet.'

Twiddle thought there was something extremely funny about bringing a sheep and a goat indoors, but he knew better than to say anything more to Mrs Twiddle. He knew he had better do as he was told at once. So he went out of doors and looked round for the sheep and the goat.

There were two sheep and a goat in the field at the bottom of his garden. Mr Twiddle sighed. The goat was tied up, but the sheep weren't. What a bother it all was! Why should Mrs Twiddle take it into her head to want to be so kind to sheep and goats all of a sudden?

Twiddle undid the gate at the bottom of the garden. He untied the goat and led it indoors to the kitchen. The goat was surprised, but it didn't mind very much. It looked at the tablecloth, and thought it might do for a meal. Twiddle shut the door and went down the garden to fetch the two sheep in out of the rain.

It was easy enough to catch one, but the other was afraid of him and ran away. So Mr Twiddle firmly led the first sheep into the kitchen, let it join the goat, and then shut the door on them. He went off to bring in the other sheep.

Now, Mrs Twiddle was lying in bed, wondering if Twiddle had brought in the sheet and the coat quickly, before they were soaked. She heard a noise in the kitchen and she called out: 'Twiddle! Twiddle!'

'Be-heeeee, hee!' said the goat pleasantly.

'Baa-haa-haa-haa!' said the sheep, nibbling at a fern in the window. Mrs Twiddle lay and listened to this in astonishment. Was Twiddle trying to be funny?

'Stop that noise,' she said sharply. 'Did you bring in the sheet and the coat, Twiddle?'

'Ba-hah!' said the sheep politely.

'Be-hee-hee,' bleated the goat.

Mrs Twiddle felt very angry. 'Twiddle! Will you please stop being funny? I don't like it when you act the goat like that! I'm asking you a question.'

'Ba-hah-haaaaa,' said the sheep wisely, and pulled over the plant-pot.

'Bee-hee-hee,' said the goat, and ate half the table-cloth. It pulled at it, and a jug of milk toppled over and fell with a crash to the floor. Mrs Twiddle lay and listened in alarm. What in the wide world was Twiddle doing? She began to think he must have gone mad.

'Twiddle! Whatever are you doing?'

She heard a pattering of feet. The goat was frightened when the milk fell over and ran round the kitchen. It bumped into the sheep who at once jumped right over two pails and a chair, making a clatter. Mrs Twiddle listened in amazement.

'Be-ha, hee, be-ha, hee!' she heard, as the goat and the sheep sang together in chorus.

'TWIDDLE! If you don't stop being funny this very minute, I'll come down and see what you're up to!' shouted Mrs Twiddle. This threat usually made Mr Twiddle stop anything, but it didn't stop the sheep or the goat. They had a very merry time chasing one another – at least, it was a merry time for the goat, who had discovered that a sheep was a nice solid thing to butt, so it kept on butting, and the sheep kept on trying to get away, and falling into everything it could.

Mrs Twiddle could bear it no longer. She got out of bed and put on her dressing-gown, telling herself all the things she would do to Twiddle when she got downstairs. She went down, with a terrible frown on her face.

The goat chose that moment to be very frisky, and when Mrs Twiddle appeared at the kitchen door, looking nice and plump and round, he thought she might be another kind of sheep. So it went up to her and butted her hard. Mrs Twiddle sat down very suddenly and screamed.

The outer door opened, and in came Twiddle with the other sheep. 'This was a most tiresome sheep to catch,' he began. 'Get in – shoo!'

The sheep gambolled in, and the goat at once butted it. The sheep backed heavily into Twiddle and he sat down just as suddenly as Mrs Twiddle had done. But Mrs Twiddle was now getting up, and there was such an awful look in her eyes that Twiddle was quite frightened.

'Twiddle! WHAT is the meaning of this?' said Mrs Twiddle, in such a terrible voice that the sheep and the goat stopped capering about, and listened too.

'Meaning of what?' asked Twiddle, from the floor. 'You told me to bring the sheep and the goat in out of the rain, didn't you?'

Mrs Twiddle stared at Twiddle as if he was quite mad. 'Twiddle – I said, bring in the *sheet* and the *coat*,' said Mrs Twiddle. 'Have you no sense? Why should I want sheep and goats in my kitchen?'

'Well, I really didn't know, dear,' said Mr

Twiddle, going very red. 'Never mind, now, never mind – you get back to bed quickly, and I'll take these creatures to the field again, I'm so very sorry about it. I must be getting a bit deaf.'

Before Mrs Twiddle could say another word – and she had plenty to say – Twiddle opened the kitchen door, and shooed out the surprised sheep and goat. They scampered down the path to the field. Twiddle slammed the kitchen door and went with them. He felt that he really couldn't bear Mrs Twiddle looking at him like that for one minute more!

He stayed out quite a long time in the rain, hoping that Mrs Twiddle would be asleep when he got in. He crept in quietly and took off his wet boots. He quietly put a few more coals on the fire. He sat down in his armchair and quietly picked up his newspaper.

'She's asleep,' he said. 'What a bit of luck! Perhaps when she wakes up, she'll think it's all a dream!'

But a voice came down the stairs at that moment.

'Twiddle! Is that you? Have you brought in the sheet and the coat as I told you?'

Well – will you believe it – Twiddle hadn't!

So out he went again into the rain and unpegged them from the line, soaking wet. And, unless I'm very much mistaken, Twiddle will be in bed with a cold himself tomorrow. And what a lot of uncomfortable things Mrs Twiddle will say to him if they both have colds in bed together! Poor old Twiddle.

## Chapter 2

# *Oh, Mr Twiddle!*

Mrs Twiddle was very busy. She had the whole table spread with all kinds of things – needles, cottons, scissors, bits of silk, flowers, and goodness knows what else!

Mr Twiddle looked at her. He badly wanted her to help him with the crossword puzzle in the newspaper, but he didn't like to ask her, because her mouth was full of pins.

'I'm always afraid she'll swallow the pins when she has so many between her lips, like that,' thought Twiddle. 'I wonder what she's doing. She has got a *mess* out on the table.'

He waited until Mrs Twiddle had taken the pins out of her mouth and used them. Then he spoke to her.

'What are you doing with all that mess on the table, dear?' he said.

'Gracious, can't you see!' said Mrs Twiddle. 'I'm putting a bit of extra trimming on my best hat. Look, it's got violets on one side, and I'm going to put these little pink roses on the other. Don't you think they'll look nice?'

'Well, it makes the hat look rather like a garden,' said Mr Twiddle. 'How long will you be?'

'I've nearly finished,' said Mrs Twiddle. 'Then I'll help you with that puzzle. I can see you're longing for a bit of help. Just go and get me that shirt of yours over there that I've washed for you. I'll sew the top button on whilst I think of it.'

Twiddle fetched his blue shirt. Mrs Twiddle quickly sewed on a button, then fluffed out the flowers on her best hat. She looked at it with pleasure.

'It's lovely,' she said. 'Now, Twiddle dear, you can do something for me whilst I clear up this mess, then I'll help you.'

'What do you want me to do?' asked Twiddle. 'Not chop wood or anything like that, I hope.'

'No,' said Mrs Twiddle. 'Just take this shirt

out and hang it on the line to dry, and take
my best hat and put it into the hat box under
my bed. By the time you've done that for me
I'll be ready.'

'Right,' said Twiddle. He picked up the
shirt and the hat and went out of the room.

Well, you know old Twiddle, don't you? So
you can guess what he did! Yes, you're right –
he took the hat out into the garden and
pegged it carefully up on the line, and he
took his blue shirt and tucked it into the hat
box under the bed!

Then he went downstairs and beamed at
his wife. She had cleared up the mess, and

143

was ready to do the puzzle with him.

'Now look,' she said, 'here's the first thing we have to guess – the name of somebody silly. Seven letters it has to be, Twiddle.'

'I know who that is!' said Twiddle, at once. 'It must be old Meddle. He's silly enough.'

'No – Meddle has six letters, not seven in his name,' said his wife. 'Guess again. Can it be Brer Rabbit – no, that's ten letters. Dear me, I can't think of the right answer at all. Let's guess the next bit.'

As they were in the middle of the puzzle there came a knock at the door and Mrs Jones put her head in and smiled at them.

'Mrs Twiddle, I'm off to tea with Sally Simple. She told me to bring you with me if you'd like to come.'

'Oh, yes, I would!' said Mrs Twiddle, jumping up at once. 'I'll just get my hat. I've finished trimming it and it looks lovely. I shall so like wearing it to Sally's.'

She rushed upstairs. She put on her best coat, found her best gloves, and then pulled out the hat box from under the bed.

She opened it – and how she stared when she saw Twiddle's blue shirt in there. 'Whatever's this in my hat box?' she cried, and she pulled out the shirt. 'Good gracious, Twiddle's mad! He's put his damp shirt into my hat box. Oh, if he's squashed it on top of my best hat I'll chase him with the rolling pin, really I will!'

She looked under the shirt, but there was no hat there. She looked on her dressing-table. No hat there. She looked on the top shelf of her wardrobe, where she kept her other hats. No – her best hat wasn't there either.

She ran downstairs to Twiddle and Mrs Jones. 'Twiddle! What did you do with my best hat? It isn't in the hat box – and you've put your shirt there! You really are a silly man.'

'But surely I put your hat there!' said Twiddle in alarm. 'Yes, surely I did. You told me to. Are you *sure* I put the shirt there? You told me to hang it on the line. I feel sure I pegged it out in the garden.'

'Well, come to the window, and we'll see if you pegged the shirt out there!' cried Mrs Twiddle, in a temper. 'Didn't I just tell you it was in the hat box! Twiddle, where did you put my best hat?'

Twiddle went to the window and looked

out into the garden, quite expecting to see his blue shirt hanging on the line, in spite of what Mrs Twiddle said. But you know what he saw, don't you? Mrs Twiddle's best hat hanging there, being blown about in the wind!

He stared at it in horror. Oh dear, oh dear, whatever in the world would Mrs Twiddle say? Mrs Twiddle saw the look of dismay on his face, and she looked out of the window, too. When she saw her lovely best hat hanging on the line she gave a scream of horror.

'Oh, you bad man! Oh, you dreadfully silly creature! You hung my best hat on the line and put your shirt in my hat box! Twiddle, you want your ears boxed! You really do! I've a good mind to do it!'

Twiddle hurried out into the garden before Mrs Twiddle could do what she said. His face was red. Why did he do things like this? Dear, dear, his wife would never forgive him for pegging out her best hat like that!

He took it in, and Mrs Twiddle snatched it from him to see if the pegs had put it out of shape. But they hadn't. She threw his blue shirt to Twiddle.

'Do what you like with it!' she cried crossly. 'It's no good my telling you to peg it on the line. Put it into the coal scuttle if you like – or inside the oven, where you once put the clock! Really, you are the silliest fellow in the world!'

Poor Twiddle said nothing. He felt most uncomfortable, because Mrs Jones was laughing. He picked up the newspaper to finish the puzzle by himself. Mrs Twiddle stood in front of the mirror and pinned on her best hat.

'It looks simply beautiful, dear,' said Mrs Jones, admiringly. 'Really, it does!'

Mrs Twiddle felt pleased. She wasn't in a temper any more. She tapped Twiddle on the shoulder.

'There's a new ginger cake for your tea in the larder,' she said. 'Finish your puzzle, and then put the kettle on to boil.'

'I wish I could guess this bit,' sighed Twiddle. 'The name of somebody silly – with seven letters!'

'I know, I know!' cried Mrs Twiddle, and she gave a little giggle.

'Who is it?' asked Twiddle.

You know what she answered, don't you! Yes, it was Mr *Twiddle*!

## Chapter 3

# *Mr Twiddle's Pear*

Once Mr Twiddle went out walking by himself, for it was a very fine day indeed. Twiddle's feet got very hot walking, and he wished he had put on his big boots. He felt very thirsty, too, and wondered if Sally Simple would let him have a drink when he passed her house.

'I'll ask her,' he thought. He walked along down the road and came to the shops. Next door to the boot shop there was a fine pear tree overhanging the street wall. On it were several green pears, nearly ripe. Mr Twiddle stared at them in delight. Now a pear to eat, a nice juicy pear when he was almost dying of thirst, would be simply lovely.

He wondered if he could call in at the boot

shop and ask the man to let him have one of the pears off the pear tree. But he didn't quite like to do that. So he stood at the door of the shop, and turned over the boots that were for sale on his big stall in front of the door.

The shopkeeper saw him and came forward. He bowed to Mr Twiddle and spoke to him politely.

'What can I do for you this morning, sir? Would you like one of those pairs.'

He meant, of course, would Twiddle like a pair of the boots and shoes he was looking at.

But Twiddle's mind was full of the pears hanging over the wall. His heart gave a jump of joy when he heard the shopkeeper say that, and he smiled all over his face.

'Would I like a pear!' he said, beaming. 'I should just think I would! How nice of you to suggest it!'

'Well,' said the shopkeeper, 'you're a very polite customer, I must say. Now, what kind of a pair would you like? What colour? Black or brown?'

Mr Twiddle felt a bit puzzled. He hadn't heard of black pears before. He thought brown ones might be a bit over-ripe. So he looked at the shopkeeper, and said: 'Well, Mr Shopkeeper, I think I'd really rather have a yellow pear, if you don't mind. I always like them best!'

The shopkeeper pursed up his lips and frowned. 'Well, I'm sorry, sir, but I haven't a single yellow pair today,' he said. 'They're all black or brown. But come in this afternoon, and maybe I'll have one for you. I can send to the other end of town to my brother. He may have a fine yellow pair.'

'Oh, pray don't bother to do that,' said Mr Twiddle. He looked at the green pears on the tree. 'Er – well, a *green* pear would do quite well, you know. They're a little bit hard, that's the only thing. Yellow ones are nice and soft.'

The shopkeeper began to think Mr Twiddle was just a little mad. 'I haven't any green pairs today,' he said gruffly. 'You come along in an hour, and I'll have a yellow pair for you. What size would you like?'

'Oh – as large as possible, please,' said Twiddle, eagerly, thinking how lovely it would be to sink his teeth into an enormous, ripe, yellow pear and taste the sweet juice.

The shopkeeper looked down at Mr Twiddle's feet. They didn't look very large to him.

'All right,' he said. 'A large, yellow pair. And would you like a laced pair or a buttoned pair?'

Mr Twiddle stared at the shopkeeper, thinking that *he* must be a little mad. He had never in his life heard of a pear with laces or buttons. After all, if you wanted to, you took the skin off a pear – you didn't unbutton or unlace it. 'He will be asking if I want hooks and eyes on it next,' thought Twiddle. 'Really, he is a most peculiar man.'

'I don't think I want my pear laced *or*

buttoned,' said Twiddle. 'Just plain, if you know what I mean.'

'I see,' said the shopkeeper, not seeing at all. 'Well – do you want a tongue?' Of course, he meant did Twiddle want a tongue inside his shoes – but Twiddle didn't know that. He stared again at the shopkeeper, and felt a little angry.

'Do I want a *tongue*?' he said. 'Well, haven't I been talking with my tongue all this time. Why should I want another. Look – here's mine! Goodbye! I'll come back in an hour's time for a nice, yellow pear, without laces or buttons and with NO tongue!'

Mr Twiddle had put out his tongue to show the shopkeeper he had one – and the shopkeeper thought he was being rude. He gazed after Twiddle, and shook his head. 'He seemed such a nice man at first,' he said. 'But he must be mad. Quite mad. Well – I'll send over to my brother's and see if he has got a nice, yellow pair of boots or shoes without laces, buttons, or tongues!'

His brother did have pair. They were bright yellow shoes with elastic sides. He was glad to get rid of them, because he hadn't been able to sell them. The shopkeeper who had talked to Twiddle looked out for him in an hour's time – and sure enough, there he was, coming back to see if he really could have a nice, juicy, yellow pear!

'Good day again!' called the shopkeeper. 'I've got that yellow pair for you – just your size, too! Look!'

Twiddle stared in dismay at the bright yellow shoes. He simply couldn't bear them. He knew Mrs Twiddle wouldn't like them either.

'Why are you offering me shoes?' he said in astonishment. 'I meant a pear to eat – you know, like those growing on that tree over there. I was thirsty. Couldn't you give me one of *those* pears? I don't want this pair of shoes. They are dreadful.'

That made the shopkeeper very angry. 'They are fine shoes!' he cried. 'You ordered them, didn't you? It's all very well for you to say you wanted a pear off that tree now – but what you asked me for was a pair of yellow shoes without laces, buttons or tongues. And here they are. Pay me for them please.'

'Now look here, now look here,' began Mr Twiddle, feeling rather frightened. 'This won't do. I'll buy a pear off your tree – but I won't buy those yellow shoes. How much will you charge me for a pear off the tree?'

'It's not my tree,' said the shopkeeper, and he looked fiercely at Twiddle. 'It doesn't grow in my garden. It grows next door. Now – what about these shoes? They cost ten pounds and they're a bargain. Pay up, please, or I'll have to go and tell that policeman over there that you've been making fun of me and won't pay my bill.'

The policeman looked a bit fierce. Twiddle gave a deep sigh and felt in his pocket. He pulled out a handful of coins and showed them to the man. 'That's all I've got,' he said.

'Well, it's fifty pence short,' said the man. 'But I'll let you off that. Do you want to put the shoes on now?'

'Oh no, thank you,' said Mr Twiddle, quickly. 'No – I'll carry them.'

So poor Twiddle went home with the bright yellow shoes and tried to hide them in the boot cupboard right at the very back. But Mrs Twiddle caught sight of them before he put them there, and called out in surprise.

'Twiddle! Are those yellow daffodils you've got? Put them in water, my dear man – don't put them in the boot cupboard!'

So poor Twiddle had to show Mrs Twiddle the shoes – and I really couldn't tell you what she said. It would fill this whole book and then want a few more pages besides! He hasn't worn the shoes yet – and I don't somehow think he ever will. He does make some funny mistakes, doesn't he?

## Chapter 4

# *Mr Twiddle and the Bulbs*

Now, one morning, when Mr Twiddle was reading his paper, Mrs Twiddle came bustling into the kitchen.

'Twiddle, when you go out shopping this morning, I want you to buy me two new bulbs, please.'

'Certainly, my dear, certainly,' said Mr Twiddle, still reading his paper.

'We'd better have big ones,' said Mrs Twiddle. 'They are much better really, though the small ones are cheaper.'

'Right,' said Mr Twiddle, still reading his paper, and not taking very much notice.

There was a clatter as Mrs Twiddle popped out to the dustbin, took off the lid, and threw something into the bin with a noise like glass.

It was the two electric light bulbs that were no good.

The kitchen one had gone, and so had the bedroom one. Mrs Twiddle did hope that Twiddle would remember to by new ones when he was out.

'I suppose you mean to read your paper till it's one o'clock and the shops are shut?' she said, after a while.

'No, my dear, certainly not,' said Mr Twiddle, hurriedly looking at the clock. 'Half-past twelve! Dear me, I'd better go. Now let me see – fish for supper, change your library book, and er-er – what else was it, dear?'

'Bulbs,' said Mrs Twiddle, banging her iron down on the table. 'BULBS, Twiddle. I knew you weren't listening to me, I knew –'

'All right, my dear, all right,' said Twiddle, and hurried off with the shopping basket before his wife could say a word more. He bought the fish, and he changed her library book, then he stood and wondered what the third thing was.

'Ah, of course – bulbs,' he said to himself. 'Now what sort of a shop do I buy bulbs at? The flower shop, I suppose. They grow bulbs

in pots and bowls, so I expect they have some
to sell loose.'

He went to the flower shop and the girl
came forward, and asked what he wanted.

'I want two bulbs,' said Mr Twiddle.

'What kind?' asked the girl. 'It's a bit late
for bulbs really, you know. You ought to have
planted them before this.'

'Oh,' said Mr Twiddle. 'Well – Mrs Twiddle
didn't say what kind she wanted. What kind
can I have?'

'Well, there are little ones, like snowdrops,' said the girl, 'and big ones, like

160

daffodils and hyacinths. And middle-size like tulips.'

'Ah – Mrs Twiddle said two big ones,' said Twiddle, remembering. 'I'll have two of your biggest, please.'

The girl picked him out two big daffodil bulbs. 'These will be a brilliant yellow,' she said. 'You will be sure to keep them nice and wet, won't you? Water them once a week in their pot.'

'Right,' said Mr Twiddle, and took the bag in which the girl had put the bulbs. He paid for them and went home, pleased that he had remembered everything.

'Well, you haven't been as long as usual,' said Mrs Twiddle. 'I suppose you didn't meet any of your friends this morning!'

'Well, no, I didn't,' said Twiddle, putting the things down on the kitchen table. 'Here's the fish – and there's the book – and there are the bulbs. I got two nice big ones.'

'Good,' said Mrs Twiddle. 'Would you like to put them in for me? One is for the kitchen and one for the bedroom.'

'I'll have to get two pots, then,' said Twiddle, and trotted out to the shed.

Mrs Twiddle stared after him in surprise.

'Did he say he'd have to get two *pots*?' she said. 'I couldn't have heard him right. After all, he has only got to stand on a chair and slip the bulb into the light for me.'

Twiddle went out and found two pots. He set a daffodil bulb in each of them. He carried them back into the house and put one pot on the kitchen window-sill and one on the sill in the bedroom.

'I've put the bulbs in for you!' he shouted to Mrs Twiddle, who was in the dining room.

'Thank you!' cried Mrs Twiddle.

'They will be a brilliant yellow,' called Mr Twiddle.

Mrs Twiddle thought he meant that the electric light bulbs would give a brilliant yellow light. 'Good,' she said, coming into the kitchen. 'We shan't need to sit in the dark now!'

Twiddle stared at Mrs Twiddle. That seemed a strange sort of remark to him, but he thought it must be a joke, so he laughed heartily. 'Ha, ha, ha!'

Mrs Twiddle didn't quite know why Twiddle was laughing, but she liked him to laugh, so she laughed, too.

'You must water them once a week,' said

Twiddle. Mrs Twiddle stopped laughing, and looked at Twiddle in surprise.

'Water *what* once a week?' she asked at last.

'The bulbs, of course,' said Twiddle.

'Don't be silly,' said Mrs Twiddle. Twiddle looked offended.

'I'm not silly,' he said. 'The girl in the shop said we were to water them once a week.'

'I don't mind you being funny, but I don't like you to be silly,' said Mrs Twiddle sharply.

'All right, all right,' said Mr Twiddle, and he said no more, thinking that probably Mrs Twiddle knew more about whether to water bulbs or not than the girl in the shop did.

Neither of them said a word more about the bulbs. But when evening came and it was dark in the kitchen Mrs Twiddle got up to switch on the electric light. Nothing happened. No light came. Mrs Twiddle looked at the light. There was no bulb there!

'I thought you said you had put the bulbs in for me,' she said to Twiddle.

'So I did, my dear; so I did,' said Twiddle, surprised.

'Well, I can't see a bulb,' said Mrs Twiddle, screwing up her eyes and looking at the light that wasn't there.

'It's on the window-sill,' said Twiddle.

'Twiddle! Why on the *window-sill*?' asked Mrs Twiddle. 'Are you mad? I can't see the bulb on the window-sill.'

'Well, only because it's in the *earth*,' said Twiddle.

'In the *earth*?' said Mrs Twiddle, wondering if Twiddle really had gone mad. 'Why should you put a bulb in the earth?'

Twiddle thought Mrs Twiddle was being terribly stupid. 'To make it grow, of course,' said Twiddle.

Mrs Twiddle looked closely at the window-sill and she saw the pot of earth there. She stared at it, and then stared at Twiddle. A funny look came over her face.

'Twiddle,' she said, 'I suppose you knew I wanted those bulbs to put into the electric lights, didn't you?'

Twiddle stared at Mrs Twiddle, and he suddenly felt very uncomfortable. Oh – how very, very awkward! So he had got the wrong kind of bulbs! Dear, dear, he was always doing things like that. Now what would Mrs Twiddle say? She would go on and on the whole of the evening.

But she didn't. She suddenly began to laugh, and when Mrs Twiddle laughed, everyone else had to laugh too, especially Twiddle.

'Oh – now I know why you wanted me to water the light once a week!' laughed Mrs Twiddle. 'Oh, Twiddle, you'll be the death of me, really you will! Well – you'll have to sit in the dark all the evening, that's all. If you *will* buy daffodil bulbs instead of electric light bulbs, I just can't help it!'

So they sat in the dark, and chuckled whenever they thought of the bright yellow daffodils that would grow from the brown bulbs. Funny old Twiddle – he does get things wrong if he can, doesn't he?

*Chapter 5*

# Mr Twiddle and the Toothpaste

Mr Twiddle cleaned his teeth well every night and morning. He had a blue tooth brush, and Mrs Twiddle had a yellow one.

Mr Twiddle liked toothpaste in a tube and Mrs Twiddle liked it in a tin. So they couldn't possibly mistake each other's brushes or toothpaste when they cleaned their teeth.

Now one night Mr Twiddle found that he had squeezed every scrap of toothpaste out of his tube. So he called to his wife from the bathroom: 'My love! Will you get me some more toothpaste tomorrow? Mine's finished.'

'I don't see why you can't remember to get it yourself,' said Mrs Twiddle. 'You pass the chemist's each morning when you fetch the paper.'

'Well, I *will* get it then,' said Twiddle.

'You'll never remember,' said Mrs Twiddle. 'I know you, Twiddle! If you had to get your own toothpaste you'd never have any to clean your teeth with for the rest of your life.'

'What an untruthful thing to say!' said Twiddle, feeling quite cross, especially as he knew it was very likely true. He did have a very bad memory. 'A most untruthful and ridiculous thing to say. I shall buy some tomorrow.'

But he didn't buy any. He passed the chemist's on his way to fetch the paper, but he didn't think about toothpaste at all, although one side of the window was filled with nothing but different kinds of toothpaste!

So, that night, he again took up the empty tube and squeezed it. 'Bother!' he thought. 'I didn't get the toothpaste! Well, I shan't say a word.'

He didn't. But Mrs Twiddle did. 'I hope your new toothpaste is all right,' she called slyly, knowing perfectly well that Twiddle hadn't bought any.

'I am going to buy some tomorrow,' said Twiddle in rather a high-and-mighty voice.

He went to get his paper as usual the next day, and when he came to the chemist's he stopped.

'Now, what was I going to buy here?' he wondered. 'What was I going to buy? A razor-blade? A bottle of cough mixture? Some blackcurrant lozenges?'

He went in and bought all of them, thinking that one of them must be right. Mrs Twiddle smiled to herself when she saw what he had bought.

'You've decided not to clean your teeth with toothpaste after all!' she said, in a polite sort of voice. 'I see you have been to the chemist's and bought quite a lot of things – but not toothpaste.'

Twiddle felt so angry with himself that he nearly boxed his own ears. He went very red and Mrs Twiddle laughed.

'I'll buy some for you myself this afternoon,' she said. So she did, because she had a very good memory, and hardly ever forgot to do what she said she would.

She came in at tea-time with her shopping in a basket. She went to put the kettle on and then she unpacked her shopping.

'There's your toothpaste,' she said, picking up a long tube. 'And here are some buns for tea. And here's a new pair of brown laces for you – and please put them into your brown shoes, not your black ones – and here's some glue to mend that broken teapot spout – and here's a new book from the library – and I've remembered to get you the soap you like.'

'Thank you, my love,' said Twiddle, wishing he had as good a memory as his wife had.

'Now do take the things that belong to you and put them away,' said Mrs Twiddle.

But, of course, Twiddle didn't. He left the laces and everything else on the side-table, and Mrs Twiddle felt quite impatient when she saw them there.

'Now he'll forget where he put the laces and the toothpaste,' she thought. 'Well, well – I shan't put the laces in his shoes for him and I shan't take his toothpaste upstairs. He really must learn to do little things for himself.

So, when Twiddle came to do his teeth again that night, once more he found that all he had on the shelf was an empty tube, quite squeezed out.

'Now let me think,' he said to himself. 'Just let me think. I *have* got some toothpaste now.

171

Mrs Twiddle got it for me. It isn't here. So it must still be downstairs on the little table. I'll go and get it before she asks me if I've cleaned my teeth.'

So Mr Twiddle crept downstairs in the dark, went to the little table in the kitchen and groped about for the toothpaste tube.

Soon he went upstairs again, very quietly, holding a tube in his hand. He didn't know he had the tube of glue instead of the tube of paste. He had quite forgotten that Mrs Twiddle had bought him some glue to mend the old teapot for her.

'Twiddle! Are you cleaning your teeth properly tonight?' called Mrs Twiddle from the bedroom.

'Yes, dear, of course! answered Twiddle, taking off the top of the tube of glue and squeezing some glue on to his tooth brush.

'Funny colour!' he thought, when he saw it. 'Not the same as usual. And what a nasty fishy smell! I wish I had gone to buy the toothpaste myself. Mrs Twiddle hasn't bought the kind I usually have.'

He began to rub his teeth with it. Oh, what a dreadful taste! Twiddle couldn't bear it. He tried to open his teeth to rinse his mouth with water. But to his amazement and horror he couldn't get his teeth apart. No wonder, because the glue was sticking them fast together!

'Twiddle! Aren't you ever coming to bed?' called Mrs Twiddle, impatiently.

'Ooogle-oo-oo,' said Twiddle, trying to say 'Just coming!' His lips seems to be sticking together now, too. Whatever could be the matter?

'What did you say, Twiddle?' called Mrs Twiddle, astonished.

'Ug-ug-ug-ug,' answered Twiddle, feeling really alarmed now.

'Twiddle! Speak up! Don't mumble like that,' said Mrs Twiddle, sharply.

'Oooph, oooph, ug,' said Twiddle, and looked at himself in the mirror in fright. Why couldn't he talk? Why couldn't he open his mouth? Whatever was happening?

'Do you think you're being funny, Twiddle?' cried Mrs Twiddle, beginning to get cross.

Twiddle didn't think he was being funny at all, but he did think he was being very strange. He worked his lips about, trying to open them. But they were stuck fast.

Mrs Twiddle jumped out of bed. She wasn't going to let Twiddle behave like that to her – mumbling and muttering instead of giving her a proper answer. She came sailing into the bathroom in her dressing-gown, looking so furious that Twiddle felt quite frightened.

'Twiddle! What is the matter with you? Answer me at once!' said Mrs Twiddle.

But that was more than poor Twiddle could do. He stared forlornly at Mrs Twiddle, and then tried to open his mouth by pulling at his stuck-together lips with his fingers, making a curious gurgling noise as he did so.

'The man's gone mad!' said Mrs Twiddle in fright. 'Oh dear – I'd better get the doctor!'

But before she went to get him she had a look round the bathroom – and there, on the shelf, lay the tube of glue, a little golden drop oozing out of the tip. Mrs Twiddle picked it up and looked at it. Then she looked at Twiddle. Then she picked up his tooth brush and felt it. The bristles stuck to her fingers!

'Twiddle,' said Mrs Twiddle. 'Oh, Twiddle! First you can't remember to buy yourself toothpaste – then I buy it for you – and yet you go and clean your teeth with the glue I bought to mend the teapot spout. Twiddle, are you mad or just plain silly? What am I to do with you?'

Twiddle stared at the tube of glue in horror. His eyes looked ready to drop out of his head. So that was why it smelt so fishy? Good gracious, he had stuck his teeth and lips together and perhaps he would never be able to get them unstuck again. Mrs Twiddle always bought such strong glue!

'You'd better come to bed before you do anything else silly,' said Mrs Twiddle. 'Come along. You'll be washing your face with the toothpaste and brushing your hair with the bathroom stool if I leave you for a moment!'

Mr Twiddle got into bed, very sad and very much alarmed. It was awful to have to listen and listen to Mrs Twiddle and not be able to answer back at all. He felt so bad about it after half an hour of listening that some big tears rolled down his cheeks.

And there must have been something very strong in poor Mr Twiddle's tears, because the drops unstuck the glue on his lips and teeth, and he was able to open his mouth again and speak! Oh, how glad he was. He sat up in bed and opened and shut his mouth like a goldfish.

'Oooph!' said Twiddle, finding his voice again. 'One more word from you Mrs Twiddle, and I get the glue and stick *your* lips together. Just one more word!'

And Mrs Twiddle was so astonished to hear Twiddle talk to her like that that she didn't say another word; so Twiddle was able to go peacefully to sleep after he had washed his lips and teeth well to get rid of the taste of glue.

But Mrs Twiddle did have the last word, of

course, the next day. She gave Twiddle the teapot to mend and handed him two tubes – the tube of toothpaste and the tube of glue.

'You probably want to use your toothpaste instead of the glue to stick on the spout,' she said, in a polite voice. 'So here are both. Use which you like.'

And that annoyed Twiddle so much that he actually thought about what he was doing, and mended the spout really well – with the glue!

## Chapter 6

# Mr Twiddle Doesn't Like the Cat

'Now, Twiddle,' said Mrs Twiddle one morning, when she had had a letter from her cousin Amanda, 'I think I shall have to go away for a day or two, because my cousin Amanda is ill and needs someone to look after her.'

'But I can't do without you,' said Twiddle, quite alarmed at being left on his own. 'Who will get my breakfast? And make the bed? And light the kitchen fire when it goes out?'

'You will, Twiddle dear,' said Mrs Twiddle. 'It's time you learnt to do a few things for yourself. It won't hurt you, and I shan't be gone long. Now, cheer up and don't look so alarmed.'

'Will you take the cat with you?' asked

Twiddle. He didn't like the cat, and the cat didn't like him. 'I don't feel as if I can possibly look after the cat.'

'Well, you must,' said Mrs Twiddle firmly. 'Of course I shan't take her with me. I shouldn't think of such a thing. Don't be silly. The cat's no trouble.'

'It's no trouble to you, but it's a great trouble to me,' said Twiddle, thinking of the many times that the cat had tripped him up, jumped on to his middle when he was asleep, and stolen fish of all kinds that he was going to have for breakfasts or suppers. 'That cat is a great nuisance. I shall not look after her.'

'You are not to talk like that, Twiddle,' said Mrs Twiddle, in such a sharp voice that Twiddle thought he really had better not say any more. But he was very upset to think that Mrs Twiddle was going away and leaving him to look after himself – and the cat.

Mrs Twiddle packed a small bag, and told Twiddle to remember ever so many things.

'The milkman has been, so there is plenty of milk for your tea. The baker will come soon. There is a herring for your supper, and a kipper for your breakfast. You know how to fry them because you have seen me do it plenty of times. There are two eggs in the larder as well, so you can have those if you want to.'

'Yes, love,' said Twiddle, trying hard to remember everything.

'And don't forget to give the cat her milk each day, and to get her into the house at night,' said Mrs Twiddle. 'And *don't* let her sleep on the beds.

'Certainly not,' said Twiddle, quite determined about that. 'Well, I hope Amanda will soon be better, my dear, so that you can come back home. I shall miss you very much.'

'Goodbye, Twiddle dear,' said Mrs Twiddle, 'and don't leave the front door open when you go out, and don't let the kitchen fire go out if you can help it, and don't leave the taps running, and don't –'

'You'll miss your bus,' said Twiddle, who didn't like all this don't-ing. 'Goodbye, love, take care of yourself.'

Mrs Twiddle went, and Twiddle trotted off into the kitchen to do the washing-up. The cat was sitting on the window-sill there, washing herself.

'You're always washing yourself,' said Twiddle. 'Can't think why. You don't get as dirty as all that. Now you listen to me, Cat – I've got to look after you – but any nonsense from you and you'll get scolded.'

'Ss-ss-sss,' said the cat, rudely.

'Don't hiss at me like that,' said Twiddle, running the hot water into the bowl. The cat watched him. Then she jumped down, rubbed against his legs, and mewed.

'What are you doing that for?' asked Twiddle. 'You only do that when you want something. You've had your milk. I saw Mrs Twiddle giving it to you.'

The cat gave up rubbing against Twiddle's legs, because he kept pushing her away. She strolled to the kitchen, which was empty. She jumped up on to the breakfast table.

The jug of milk was still there. The cat began to lick, trying her hardest to reach the milk. When she had licked a little of it, she put up her paw to try and get the milk nearer – and over went the jug!

The milk streamed over the table. The cat was pleased. Now there was plenty! She began to lick it up.

Twiddle heard the noise of the falling jug and came to see what it was. He was very angry when he saw the spilt milk and the spoilt table cloth. He tried to smack the cat, but she put out a paw and gave him a sharp scratch, then leapt out of the window.

'Bother the thing!' said Twiddle, annoyed. He bathed the scratch, and then went on with the washing-up. When he had done that he tidied the kitchen, and swept the washroom. Then he felt very tired and went to sit down in his armchair. He took up the paper – but he didn't read much of it because he was soon asleep. Mrs Twiddle said that Twiddle could go to sleep at any hour of the day, and this was quite true.

Twiddle was really enjoying his nap when

something landed with a jerk right on his middle, and then settled down heavily, digging pins into him all the time. He woke up with a jump.

The cat was lying peacefully on him, digging her claws in and out, purring loudly, very comfortable and happy. Twiddle was very angry. He tried to shake the cat off, but she clung to him with all her claws.

'How many times have I told you not to jump on me like that?' shouted Twiddle, in a fine old rage. 'You make me into a sort of bed for yourself, and always wait till I'm asleep before you jump. I won't have it!'

He shook the cat off at last, shooed her to the door and slammed it behind her. Then he settled down again. But the cat came in at the window, waited by the fire till Twiddle was sound asleep and snoring a little, and then jumped up on to his meddle once more. Twiddle awoke again with a jump, and the cat leapt off.

Poor Twiddle! He decided not to sleep any more. The cat didn't mean to let him, anyway. Twiddle went to the fridge and wondered what to have for his dinner. The baker came whilst he was wondering, and Twiddle went to get the bread from him. He left the larder door open.

The cat went in, and smelt the herring and jumped up to the shelf at once. The next thing that Twiddle saw was the cat dragging his precious herring over the floor and out of the door. He was just too late to stop her.

'Look at that cat!' he said to the baker. 'She's the most annoying, interfering cat you ever saw. I suppose you don't want a cat, do you?'

'Well, I've rats in the bakery,' said the

baker. 'I don't mind having her. If she'll catch them I'll keep her.'

'Well, you can have her and welcome,' said Twiddle. He ran after the cat, pounced on her and popped her into a box. The baker put her into his van and drove off. Twiddle was very pleased.

'Now that cat can't interfere with me any more, he said, rubbing his hands together. 'I shall have to have the kipper for my supper, now that she has stolen the herring. And I'll have an egg for my breakfast.'

Twiddle thought it was very nice without the cat. He could leave the larder door open if he wanted to. He could leave the milk on the table. He could go to sleep without being woken up with a jump.

When his supper-time came he cooked the kipper.

It smelt good. He put it on a plate and carried it carefully to the kitchen. But suddenly he tripped over something and fell down with a crash. The plate broke. The kipper shot into the air and disappeared. Twiddle banged his head hard against the wall.

'Miaow!' said a voice, and Twiddle saw the

cat sitting down in the passage, looking at him.

'So it was *you* that tripped me up, was it?' said Twiddle, very angry, and most surprised to see the cat there after he had given it to the baker. 'What have you come back again for? Hi – leave that kipper alone!'

The cat had suddenly smelt the kipper, which had landed on a nearby chair. She jumped up and pounced on it. She fled out of the door with it.

'Well, it looks as if I'm never going to have any meals in this house whilst that cat's about,' thought poor Twiddle. 'Herring gone – kipper gone – it's too bad.'

Twiddle was so angry that when it was time to lock up the house, he didn't open the door and call the cat in, as he usually did. No – let her stay out in the cold, the horrid, thieving animal! She ought to be sitting in the bakery, catching mice.

So the cat was left out and Twiddle went to bed. He fell asleep and had an awful dream. He dreamt that somebody made him lie down flat on the ground and then piled bricks on his tummy, higher and higher. Poor Twiddle woke up suddenly, and wondered what the heavy weight was on the top of him.

The cat of course! She had jumped in at the bedroom window, meaning to go downstairs and find her basket. But the bedroom door was shut and she couldn't. So she had jumped up on to Twiddle and settled down there, warm and comfortable.

'Well, that's the last straw!' said Twiddle, in a rage, heaving the cat off the bed. 'Tomorrow I sell you. Yes, I do. I sell you. So make up your mind to it, Cat – you're going to be sold.'

Twiddle meant what he said. The cat managed to trip him up twice the next day, and then Twiddle caught her, and put her into a box. He shut down the lid, tied it with string and set off.

He walked about two miles and came to a small cottage where there lived an old woman who was very fond of cats. She had once been to tea with Mrs Twiddle, and had taken such a fancy to the cat that she had offered to buy it. But Mrs Twiddle wouldn't sell her.

It didn't take Twiddle long to sell the cat to the old woman. He got five pounds for her, and was very pleased. He thought he would spend the money on beautiful roses to put in

Mrs Twiddle's bedroom. So he stopped at the flower shop and bought a pretty bunch of red and pink ones.

When he got home he found a telegram from Mrs Twiddle. 'Amanda is better. Returning home this afternoon.'

'Good,' thought Mr Twiddle, pleased. He set to work to clean the house and make it nice for Mrs Twiddle. He went out and bought a meat pie and some tarts. He put the roses into water, and they made the bedroom smell beautiful.

Mrs Twiddle came home and was pleased to see everything looking so nice, and she simply loved the roses. 'Oh, how beautiful!' she cried. 'How kind of you, Twiddle dear. But where did you get the money from? They must have cost quite a lot of money.'

Twiddle suddenly felt that he didn't want to explain about selling the cat. He cleared his throat, smiled rather nervously, and stared at Mrs Twiddle.

'I might have sold the cat, mightn't I?' he said, with a queer little laugh.

'Of course, you wouldn't do a thing like that!' said Mrs Twiddle. 'What, be so cruel and unkind as to sell my dear, darling old puss-cat that I love? Don't be silly, Twiddle. You know if you did a thing like that I'd chase you out of the house with my umbrella, and not let you in again till you brought the cat back.'

This was very alarming. Twiddle had had no idea that Mrs Twiddle would feel like this about the cat. He went very red and felt frightened.

'But I'm sure you haven't sold the cat. You've bought me some lovely, lovely roses out of your own money,' said Mrs Twiddle, and she gave poor Mr Twiddle a big kiss. 'And now where is puss? I thought she'd be here to greet me.'

Twiddle began to tremble, thinking that surely he would be chased out of the house with an umbrella in a minute or two. And then a most surprising thing happened.

The cat ran in at the door, went straight to Mrs Twiddle, rubbed against her skirt, and made some very loving noises.

'You darling. You came to greet me, after all. Where were you? Did you know that Twiddle said he might have sold you! Isn't he a naughty story-teller?'

Twiddle was very thankful to see the cat, but dear, dear, how was he going to make it up to the old woman who had bought her. The cat must have run away from her and come all the way home. She would be sure to come and call and ask if the cat had come back.

'There's only one thing to be done,' thought Twiddle gloomily. 'I must empty my pockets, and see if I have enough money. I must take it to her and say the cat is back. Then perhaps Mrs Twiddle will never know how foolish I have been.'

So poor Twiddle took back most of his

pocket-money to the old woman who had bought the cat.

He couldn't buy any tobacco, sweets or papers for a week. Poor Twiddle. I don't suppose he'll ever really like the cat now, do you?

## Chapter 7

# *Mrs Twiddle's Necklace*

Mrs Twiddle had a sister called Julia, and one day, on Mrs Twiddle's birthday, Julia sent her a bead necklace.

Mrs Twiddle was delighted with it. She showed it proudly to Twiddle.

'Look, Twiddle,' she said. 'Did you ever see such dear little beads? All different colours, and all sizes and shapes! Julia must have threaded this pretty necklace herself. She always was a clever one with her hands.'

'Very nice, dear, very nice indeed,' said Twiddle. 'It will look beautiful with the new dress I have given you.'

It did. It went with it very nicely, and Mrs Twiddle enjoyed going out to tea in her new dress, wearing the string of tiny, coloured beads round her neck. She was really very proud of her new necklace, and liked it very much.

One day, just as she was going out shopping, the necklace broke! Mrs Twiddle was dreadfully upset. Some of the beads were left on the string but most of them went tumbling and bouncing all over the floor.

'Oh, look at that now!' said Mrs Twiddle in dismay. 'Twiddle, come and pick them up for me, quick! I can't stop or I shall miss the bus.'

'Certainly, love, certainly,' said Twiddle, folding up his newspaper carefully and getting out of his chair. 'Dear, dear, what a pity! But don't you worry now – I'll find every one of the beads, and you can take them to the jeweller's and get them properly re-threaded.

'Twiddle, be sure you put them somewhere safe when you've found them all,' said Mrs Twiddle, putting on her hat. 'Now don't you put them somewhere silly, where I shall never find them. Put them in the little jug on the dresser. That would be a good place for them.'

'All right, dear,' said Twiddle, busy hunting for the beads on the floor. 'Goodbye. Don't miss the bus. I'll have all the beads found and put away safely by the time you come back.'

Mrs Twiddle hurried off to catch her bus. Twiddle went on looking for the beads. It was astonishing how far they had bounded and rolled.

The cat came strolling in as he was hunting for them, and was astonished, but pleased, to find Twiddle on all-fours on the floor. She had an idea he meant to play with her, so she playfully leapt at him, knocking about twenty beads out of his hand as she did so.

'Just the sort of silly thing you *would* do!'

said Twiddle, staring at the cat in disgust. 'Go away. I never knew such a cat for coming in when it wasn't wanted. Go and catch mice!'

The cat understood the word 'mice' and ran abut excitedly looking for one, getting in Twiddle's way in a most annoying manner. Every time he put his hand under the sofa or chair to get a bead the cat put out her paw and patted him, so that he kept dropping the bead.

'Go away!' he said to the cat. 'Who can pick up beads with you bothering round like this? My gracious, what a lot there are all over the place. I shall never find them all with you gambolling round.'

The cat felt that Twiddle was not really pleased with her company, and she strolled out, tail in air. Twiddle was glad. Now he could find the beads quickly, put them away, and sit down to read his paper.

He found all he could, and stood up with them safe in his hand. Now, where did Mrs Twiddle tell him he could put them?

'Ah – in that jug on the dresser, of course,' said Twiddle. He went to the dresser, reached up, and popped all the beads into the jug. But they didn't make the little rattling noise he expected to hear. So he reached down the jug and looked into it.

It was half-full of milk! Bother! Now he would have to empty the milk into the flat plate and scrape out all the beads and dry them. Mrs Twiddle wouldn't be at all pleased to see them swimming in the milk.

So Twiddle poured the milk into a flat enamel plate and then went to get a spoon to scrape out the beads.

The cat came in whilst he was getting the spoon, and saw the milk in the plate. How nice of Twiddle to set out so much milk for her, she thought. She jumped up on the table and began lapping it.

Twiddle heard her, and was angry. He shooed her away. 'You again! Always interfering! I suppose you've swallowed half the beads!'

The cat thought that Twiddle was most unreasonable that afternoon. She went to the window-sill, sat down in the sun, and began to wash herself slowly and thoroughly, watching Twiddle out of one of her bright green eyes as she did so.

'Stare all you like, silly animal,' said Twiddle, who was not fond of the cat. 'It's not my fault the beads went into the milk. It's Mrs Twiddle's. She should have remembered there was milk in the jug.'

Twiddle got all the beads out and carefully dried them. He emptied the milk back again into the jug, spilling quite a lot on the floor as he did so.

'You can lick that up,' he told the cat. 'It will save me getting a cloth to wipe up the mess.'

But the cat had had enough of Twiddle that afternoon. She felt quite certain that as soon as she leapt down to lap up the spilt milk Twiddle would send her away again. So she took no notice and went on washing herself.

'You really are a most annoying and disobedient cat,' said Twiddle. 'Most disobliging. Now I've got to wipe up the mess myself.'

When he had wiped it up he stared at the little pile of beads. What should he do with them? Where would a safe place be?

He looked at the dresser. What about putting them in another jug? But there was no jug there. They were all in the larder.

'Well, what about the teapot? That's an even better place,' thought Twiddle, and he took it down from the shelf.

He put the beads into it, then put on the lid. 'There now! They are perfectly safe. Isn't that good?'

He took up his newspaper, sat down in his chair, and began to read. He had a very peaceful time till Mrs Twiddle came back. She brought her sister Julia with her.

'Hello, Twiddle dear,' said Mrs Twiddle. 'Wasn't it lucky, I met Julia and told her I'd broken my necklace, and she said she'd come back and have tea with us and thread the beads again herself. Now, wasn't that kind of her?'

'Oh, very,' said Twiddle. 'Very kind indeed. Shall I put the kettle on to boil, dear?'

'No, I'll do that,' said Mrs Twiddle, who knew that Twiddle would probably put the kettle on and forget to light the gas. 'You show Julia the beads and get out my work-basket so that she can get the needle and thread ready to mend the necklace after tea.'

Twiddle gave Julia the work-basket, and then looked round for the beads. Where had he put them?

'The beads, Twiddle,' said Julia. 'Where are they?'

'What did you do with them?' asked Mrs Twiddle. 'Did you put them into that jug?'

'Oh, yes, I did,' said Twiddle. 'But wait a minute – the jug had milk in it so I had to take out the beads after all. It was such a business.'

'Well, where did you put the beads after that?' said Mrs Twiddle, impatiently.

The cat looked at Twiddle as if it could tell him. Twiddle looked at the cat. But he simply could not remember where he had put those beads! He felt in his pockets. He looked in the little jar on the mantelpiece where odds-and-ends were often put. He opened the desk and looked there.

'Oh, Twiddle, for goodness' sake stop fiddling about and find the beads!' said Julia. 'You *must* know where you put them!'

The cat knew, but Twiddle still didn't. He really had a very bad memory indeed.

'Oh, let's have tea and perhaps Twiddle will remember by that time,' said Julia.

'Here's the teapot,' said Twiddle, anxious to help. He took the teapot to the stove, and stood it there to warm it.

Mrs Twiddle took off the lid and popped in four spoonfuls of tea. Then she poured the boiling water in.

'Nice hot cup of tea!' she said. 'It will do us all good.'

They sat down to tea. There was bread-and-butter and jam, and some nice new chocolate buns. Twiddle felt that he was really going to enjoy his tea.

'Sugar and milk, Julia?' asked Mrs Twiddle, and put them both into Julia's cup. Then she poured out the tea, and Twiddle handed the cup to Julia.

Then Mrs Twiddle poured out Twiddle a

cup of tea and then one for herself. The beads came rushing out of the spout with the tea, and settle down at the bottom of each cup.

Everyone took sugar so they had to stir their tea. Twiddle stirred his sharply, and then gazed at it in astonishment. All kinds of little, round, coloured things surged round and round the surface as he stirred it.

'What are they?' thought Twiddle. 'Bubbles?'

Julia also stirred her tea and looked down

at it in surprise. As for Mrs Twiddle, she was really alarmed.

'Don't drink the tea!' she cried. 'There's something wrong with it – insects or something! Goodness gracious, how disgusting!'

Twiddle stared down at his cup – and an awful thought came into his head. Beads! He had put the beads into the teapot for safety! And he had forgotten. So Mrs Twiddle had made tea out of tea leaves, hot water – and beads! Now what would she say?

Mrs Twiddle got some of the beads into her spoon and stared at them in astonishment and anger.

'My *beads*!' she said. 'Why, they're my *beads*!'

'Well – just fancy that – so they are!' said Twiddle.

'How *did* they get into the tea?' said Julia, in surprise. 'Are there any in the teapot, dear?'

Whilst Mrs Twiddle was looking, Twiddle got up very quickly and left the room. He went into the garden and sat down in the woodshed. He felt that he knew everything that Mrs Twiddle and Julia would say. He really didn't want to hear it. It was a pity to miss his tea, but the woodshed would be much more peaceful than the kitchen.

The cat walked in and stared at Twiddle. It made him angry. 'You go away!' said Twiddle 'Just come to gloat over me, haven't you? Well, you go and tell Mrs Twiddle and Julia that they're always making a fuss about nothing and I'm NOT GOING TO STAND IT. See?'

But the cat wasn't bold enough to say anything like that to Mrs Twiddle! No – she just sat there waiting for Mrs Twiddle to come and fetch Mr Twiddle in. She knew there would be some fun then!

## Chapter 8

# Mr Twiddle and the Tickets

Mr and Mrs Twiddle were going away for a holiday. What fun!

'Now I'll do all the packing,' said Mrs Twiddle. 'If you do it you'll take the most ridiculous things and leave out all the ones we shall really want.'

'No, I shan't,' said Twiddle, feeling hurt.

'Well, don't you remember last time you did the packing?' said Mrs Twiddle. 'You packed the kitchen poker and although it was summer time, you packed all your winter vests. I never did know why you packed the poker.'

'Only because I thought it might come in useful,' said Mr Twiddle. 'You never know when or where you might meet a burglar.'

'Well – I'll do the packing this time,' said Mrs Twiddle, 'and then we shall be certain of our tooth brushes and night clothes and hankies and things like that. I'll ask Julia, my sister, if she'll have the cat whilst we're away.

'I'm glad we're not going to pack the cat, anyway,' said Twiddle, who thought their cat was a most interfering nuisance. He was always falling over her.

'And I'll shut up the house and tell the milkman not to leave any milk,' went on Mrs Twiddle.

'It seems to me as if you're going to do everything and leave me nothing to do at all,' said Mr Twiddle. 'Can't I do *any*thing?'

'Yes – you can go and buy the railway tickets,' said Mrs Twiddle. 'And mind you put them somewhere safe so that you don't lose them.'

So Twiddle went to buy the tickets. He put them into his pocket – nice green tickets that would take him and Mrs Twiddle to the seaside for a lovely holiday. Mr Twiddle enquired about the trains.

'There's one at ten o'clock and one at eleven,' said the porter. 'You had better be here ten minutes before the train goes, with your luggage, then I can get you good corner seats.'

'Right,' said Twiddle. 'Thank you very much.'

He went home. 'I've got the tickets, dear,' he said, and he showed her them. 'So we shan't have to get them on the day. That will save us a minute or two.'

'Where are you going to put them?' asked Mrs Twiddle. 'Don't put them into the teapot, please, where you once put my beads. I couldn't bear to drink ticket-tea.'

'Of course I shan't do a thing like that,' said Twiddle, crossly. 'I shall put them somewhere very safe indeed.'

'Well, for goodness' sake tell me where you are going to put them,' said Mrs Twiddle, 'because you are sure to forget, and I shall have to remind you.'

Twiddle looked round the kitchen. Should he put them into the picture frame.

'No,' he thought. 'Mrs Twiddle might go dusting there and flick them out.'

He looked round again. Should he put them inside the clock? He wound the clock up every night, and he could see them there each time, and be reminded where they were.

'No. That won't do either,' he thought. 'Mrs Twiddle is always talking of sending the clock to be mended. It would be awful if she did send it, and the tickets, too. Dear me, where *can* I put them?'

Then he thought he would put them into his hat-band. They would be safe there because his hat-band was very tight, and he would see them every time he went out. He went to put them there, but then he changed his mind.

'No. It might rain when I was out, then the tickets would get wet and soft,' he thought. 'Oh, dear – where can I put these silly railway tickets? I wish I hadn't gone and got them.'

Well, in the end, Twiddle decided that the very safest place of all would be in his waistcoat pocket! Then he would be bound to take them to the station with him, because he would be wearing his waistcoat, anyhow!

'Have you found a place for the tickets, Twiddle?' asked Mrs Twiddle, at last. Twiddle nodded.

'Yes,' he said. 'A very sensible place, too. In my waistcoat pocket.'

'Good,' said Mrs Twiddle. 'You simply can't

help taking them with you if you put them there.'

Mrs Twiddle soon started her packing and finished it. She got Twiddle to sit on the trunk whilst she strapped it up. She went to her sister Julia's with the cat. But when she got home again the cat was there before her. She didn't like Julia.

'It's a very silly cat, the way it behaves,' said Twiddle, in disgust. 'It's not a bit of good you taking her to Julia's. She will keep on and on coming back. Can't she catch mice and rats for herself? She always seems to me to look after herself very well.'

But Mrs Twiddle didn't like the idea of leaving the cat without anyone to see to her. So once more she took her round to Julia, and this time she was locked in the scullery, and was not able to get home before Mrs Twiddle did.

The great morning came. Mr and Mrs Twiddle had an early breakfast, shut up the house, and got into the taxi that called for them.

On the way to the station Mrs Twiddle asked Twiddle to get the tickets ready. He felt round for them.

But what was this – he hadn't got his waistcoat on! He was wearing his pullover instead! Mrs Twiddle stared at Twiddle in dismay.

'You stupid man! You decided to wear your pullover instead of your waistcoat – and now you must have gone and left the tickets behind. Quick – tell the taxi driver to go back.'

Twiddle rapped on the window and told

the driver to turn and go back. He felt very cross with himself. They got to the house and Twiddle jumped out. He unlocked the front door and went in. He ran up the stairs and went to the wardrobe.

His waistcoat was there. Twiddle ran his fingers into the pockets and gave a loud groan. There were no tickets there!

'My, my, my!' said Twiddle. 'What have I done with them? Now I come to think of it I did take them out when I took off the waistcoat and decided to put on my pullover! But where did I put them?'

He felt in all his pockets. He looked in his hat-band. He looked in his shoes!

No tickets. He heard Mrs Twiddle calling out to him. 'Twiddle, Twiddle! What in the world are you doing? Do you want to miss the train? For goodness' sake come along.'

'Coming, coming!' yelled Mr Twiddle, and hurriedly looked all round the bedroom for the tickets. He looked in the drawers. No tickets. He looked on the wash stand. No tickets. He looked under the bed. Certainly no tickets.

'TWIDDLE! It's ten to ten. You MUST come!' called Mrs Twiddle, and the taxi driver hooted his horn so loudly that all the neighbours looked out of their windows in surprise.

'JUST coming!' yelled poor Twiddle, and went down the stairs three steps at a time. He ran into the kitchen. He must have put the tickets there.

He looked inside the clock. No tickets. He looked in the picture frame. No tickets. He even looked inside the teapot, the milk jug and the sugar basin. But there were no tickets to be seen anywhere.

Mrs Twiddle got out of the cab and came hastily into the house. 'Twiddle! What are you doing? Why don't you come? We shall certainly miss the train.'

'I can't find the tickets,' said poor Twiddle, his face as red as a beetroot.

'Toot-toot-toot!' went the taxi driver's horn.

Mrs Twiddle made a clicking noise that Twiddle hated, because it always meant that she felt very cross.

'I might have guessed it!' she said. 'The one thing I asked you to do! Was there ever a sillier man than you? Well, well – you have probably put them down the sink, or in the dustbin, or even on the rubbish heap, so it's no good looking for them. Come along. We shall have to buy some more.'

Mr Twiddle slammed the front door. He went out to the taxi, and as he went he saw something lying on the garden wall. It was the cat.

'Look at that,' he said to Mrs Twiddle. 'There's the cat back again. I hope you won't take her to Julia's again.'

'Oh, dear,' said Mrs Twiddle, in dismay. 'No, we haven't time. She must go with us! I am sure she would sit quietly on your knee all the time.'

'What! Take that cat with us – on my knee!' cried Twiddle, horrified. 'You know she doesn't like me. Why, part of the niceness of having a holiday was leaving that cat behind. She's always interfering with me.'

'Well, Puss will have to come,' said Mrs Twiddle firmly. 'Hold your tongue, Twiddle. What with losing the tickets, and missing the train, you've done enough for one morning.'

The train could be heard in the distance. It had come into the station and was now on its way out. How tiresome! They really had missed it.

'Train's gone, ma'am,' said the taxi driver.

'I know,' said Mrs Twiddle. 'Twiddle, take the

cat, please. I've got the lunch basket to carry.'

'I'll carry the basket,' said Twiddle. 'You carry the cat.'

'No. You'd lose the lunch things,' said Mrs Twiddle. 'Here's the cat. You can't lose *her* – she'll be frightened and stick close to you.'

They arrived at the station. 'I must go and buy some new tickets,' said Mrs Twiddle. 'Now, hold on to the cat and stand just here, so that I know where you are.'

Mrs Twiddle went to the ticket office. She opened her bag to get out her money – and there, neatly tucked in among the coins were two green railway tickets! Mrs Twiddle stared at them.

'The tickets!' she said. 'They're in my bag! How in the world did they get there?'

She hurried back to Twiddle, who was trying to stop the cat from putting her claws into his shoulder.

'Twiddle! Look here! How did these tickets get into my bag?'

Twiddle stared – and then he grinned in delight.

'Of course! That is where I put them when I changed my waistcoat for a pullover! I remember thinking that the very safest place of all would be your bag, because you are never parted from that, and you would be sure to take it to the station with you. Wasn't I clever, dear?'

'It would have been cleverer to remember where you had put them,' said Mrs Twiddle. 'We have missed the train. But never mind – the porter says there is another at eleven o'clock, and it's faster than the one we missed and won't be so crowded. And anyway it was a good thing we had to go back, because we found poor old Puss, and she'll be able to have a holiday with us.'

'Oh my!' groaned Twiddle to himself. 'Why didn't I remember I'd popped the tickets into Mrs Twiddle's bag? Then we wouldn't have gone back and found the cat. Now she'll spoil my holiday, I know she will! In future I'll be sensible and remember every single thing!'

But he won't, will he! Poor old Twiddle. He had the cat on his knee all the way to the seaside, and dear me, how she did dig her twenty claws into him!

## Chapter 9

# Mr Twiddle and the Snow

It was a very snowy day. Mr Twiddle hoped that Mrs Twiddle wouldn't want him to go out in it. It was difficult to walk in thick snow, and Mr Twiddle felt he would much rather sit by the fire and read the paper.

But soon he heard Mrs Twiddle's voice. 'I hope you are not going to sit indoors this fine day, Twiddle. The sun is out now. It will do you good to go out. Will you fetch me some fish from the fishmonger's?'

Twiddle groaned. He knew he would have to. He put on his galoshes and his coat and hat, took a basket and set out. The children were having a fine time that day. They were making snowballs and throwing them, they were building snowmen, and they were

217

sliding down the big hill nearby on sledges.

Mr Twiddle had quite a time dodging snowballs and sledges. Then he stood still and watched some children at the top of the hill, making a very big snowball indeed.

'We're going to roll it down the hill and it will get bigger and bigger,' they cried. Mr Twiddle watched as they began to roll the big ball downwards.

Half-way down it was very big indeed. Then it began to roll down by itself, like a round avalanche. It came down more and more quickly, and Twiddle tried to hop out of the way. But he was just too late and the great big snowball struck him very hard indeed.

Mr Twiddle was knocked right over. Then he was taken onwards with the snowball, which was still rolling and gathering more snow. On and on he went, rolling over and over, getting the snow all round him. Then the snowball stopped, in the middle of the village street, which just then happened to be empty.

'Didn't it roll well!' shouted the children on the hill. 'Let's make another.'

They hadn't seen that their snowball had knocked down and taken Mr Twiddle along with it. They set to work to make another.

Mr Twiddle was buried in the middle of the big snowball. He didn't like it. He had snow down his neck, and in his mouth, ears, and nose. It was cold and horrid. Mr Twiddle began to struggle and groan.

An old lady came by and she looked in alarm at the snowball. What peculiar noises were coming out of it! What was the matter with it?

'Grrrrrrrr,' said Twiddle, growling with anger in the middle of the snowball, trying to get his head out. A little dog came up and barked in excitement.

The old lady hurried off to tell a policeman. 'There's a snowball behaving in a very strange manner,' she told him. 'Right in the middle of the village street. It said "Grrrrrrr" just like a dog.'

'I'll look into the matter,' said the policeman, looking surprised. He went off to the snowball and looked at it. What a big one! And what noises came from it. He scratched his head and wondered if he ought to arrest a snowball.

Presently some more people came up and looked at the snowball, which was now wriggling a bit here and there, and was still making strange noises.

'What is it?' said everyone. 'Is there some animal inside? Who put the snowball here?'

Suddenly out shot Mr Twiddle's head, and he blinked round at everyone in surprise. The policeman jumped and stared. Why, this must be some sort of a snowman! He took out his notebook.

'How did you get into the snow? Are you pretending to be a snowman? Did you build the snow up all round yourself?' cried the people, in surprise.

'Help me out,' said Mr Twiddle. 'I've lost my glasses in the snow.'

'I'll have to arrest you for obstructing the traffic,' said the policeman, and wrote in his notebook.

'How can I obstruct traffic when there isn't any?' said Twiddle, indignantly, trying to get his arms out of the snowball.

'Well, you would have obstructed it if there had been any,' said the policeman. 'You come along with me.'

'How can I? I'm in the middle of this big

snowball,' said Twiddle. 'Do you suppose I like being here? Nobody helps me at all!'

'Well, you got yourself in, so I suppose you can get yourself out,' said the policeman.

'When I get out I'm going to tell you a few things,' said Twiddle, angrily, 'and I shouldn't be a bit surprised to find myself pulling your nose!'

'Now, now, look here, you can't talk to the police like that!' said the policeman, crossly. 'As soon as you're out of that snowball I'm going to take you straight to the police station!'

That made Twiddle feel upset. He didn't want to be marched off to the police station. What would Mrs Twiddle say if she heard he was locked up? He would never hear the last of it.

He stopped trying to get out of the big snowball. Perhaps if he stayed there quietly the policeman would get tired of waiting and would go away. But he didn't. He began to scrape at the snow to free Twiddle. He badly wanted to take him off to the police station now. He would show Twiddle that he couldn't talk about pulling noses!

Goodness knows what would have happened if the children at the top of the hill hadn't sent down another enormous snowball! It came bounding down the hill, getting bigger and bigger as it came. It shot into the village street, and arrived at top speed just where the crowd stood, watching Twiddle.

In a second everyone was bowled over, and buried in the snow, for the snowball burst all over them. The policeman was right underneath. He lost his helmet, his note-book and his temper.

As soon as Twiddle saw everyone on the

ground, groping about wildly, he saw his chance of escape. He struck out at the snow surrounding him, managed to get free, found his glasses, and rushed off home. He didn't stop till he got there. Then he put on his glasses, brushed down his coat, and went indoors.

'Well,' he thought, as he sat down in his chair and picked up the paper, 'well – I'm not going out again today for anyone in the world! What a time I've had! Nearly buried in snow – almost taken off to prison – well, well, well.'

'Is that you, Twiddle?' called Mrs Twiddle. 'Put the fish in the larder, will you?'

Twiddle frowned and rubbed his nose. He had forgotten all about the fish! Now what was he to do? Well, he wouldn't say anything at all, and perhaps Mrs Twiddle wouldn't notice the fish wasn't there, till the next day when she wanted to cook it.

But she did notice it. She went to the larder to cut a bit off the fish for the cat – and to her surprise there was no fish there!

'Twiddle! There's no fish! The cat must have had it! How many times have I told you not to leave the larder door open?'

'About six hundred times,' said Twiddle, politely.

'Don't be rude,' said Mrs Twiddle. 'Well, what a waste – to think all that fish is inside the cat. Go and put on your hat and coat and fetch some more.'

Twiddle groaned. He went to fetch his hat and coat and then Mrs Twiddle appeared too, dressed ready to go out. 'It's such a nice afternoon,' she said. 'I thought I would come with you.'

'Well, if you're going out, I may as well stay at home,' said Twiddle, pleased, and took off his hat. But no, he had to go, to keep Mrs Twiddle company.

On the way they met the policeman, who had a black eye because someone had kicked him by accident when they had all been knocked over by the snowball. Mrs Twiddle was very sorry to see it.

'Ah,' said the policeman, stroking his eye gently. 'Ah, I had a bad time this morning. I was just about to make an arrest of a man who was obstructing the traffic and being very rude to me, when a big snowball knocked me down, and my prisoner escaped.'

'What bad luck!' said Mrs Twiddle. 'Fancy

the man being rude to you! I wonder that he dared to.'

'He said he would pull my nose,' said the policeman. Mrs Twiddle clicked her tongue in horror, and then walked on with Twiddle, who hadn't said a word all the time.

'Would you believe it!' said Mrs Twiddle, in a tone of horror. 'Well, Twiddle, silly though you are sometimes, I'm quite sure *you* would never be rude to a policeman.'

And still Twiddle never said a word. Well, there wasn't anything he could say! Poor Twiddle.

### Chapter 10

# Mr Twiddle Isn't Very Helpful

Mr Twiddle was out shopping. He had a list of things to buy, which Mrs Twiddle had written out for him. She said he would never remember any of them if she didn't, and she was quite right, he would not remember.

'I've got a visitor coming,' she said to Mr Twiddle. 'A brother of my best friend. So be sure you bring everything back with you, Twiddle, and I can give him a nice lunch.'

Twiddle went to the grocer's. Beside him was a dear old lady, and on the floor beside her was a shopping bag, quite full. Next to her was a big, burly fellow, buying all kinds of things.

The old lady was served and she went out of

the shop. It was Twiddle's turn next and he began to read from his list. 'Half a pound of bacon. One pound of sugar. A pot of strawberry jam.'

And then Twiddle saw on the floor, near him the shopping bag, quite full! He stared at it. Why, that dear old lady must have gone off without her bag! How upset she would be.

'Excuse me a minute,' said Twiddle to the surprised shop-girl. He snatched up the bag, and hurried out of the shop, leaving his list on the counter till he came back.

'I must catch up that dear old lady!' he thought. 'I really must. Poor old thing – how worried she will be when she finds she hasn't got her shopping!'

The old lady was right away in the distance. 'She walks fast,' thought Twiddle, and set off after her. He almost ran, because he was so anxious to catch her up.

He hadn't gone very far before he heard a shout behind him. He turned round and saw the shop-girl and the big, burly man both yelling and waving to him. 'Oh, dear – I suppose they're telling me they have found my shopping list and want me to go back for it!' thought Mr Twiddle. He stood still and shouted back.

'I'll be back in a minute!' Then on he went again, running to catch up the old lady.

The big, burly man set out after Mr Twiddle. 'Hi!' he yelled. 'You come back! Hi!'

Mr Twiddle thought the man was foolish. He might guess he would be coming back soon! So he took no notice and hurried on. The man hurried, too.

'You wait till I catch you!' yelled the man. 'You just wait!'

Twiddle thought that was a bit peculiar.

Why should he be caught? What did the man mean? He must be a little mad.

Twiddle went faster, taking a look now and again over his shoulder. The man looked hot and angry.

'I'll shake you till your teeth rattle!' yelled the man. 'I'll pull your ears! I'll . . .'

Twiddle felt really alarmed. Why was this man so annoyed? He really must be quite mad. Twiddle ran so fast that he panted like an engine going uphill.

Suddenly he felt a heavy hand on his shoulder, and he was pulled to a stop. The big, burly man swung little Mr Twiddle round and glared at him.

'Hand over that bag!' he said, angrily.

'Certainly not,' said Twiddle. 'It's not yours. This is robbery!'

'It certainly is – but you're the robber!' said the man, very red in the face. 'Give me that bag.'

'I shall not,' said Twiddle. 'It belongs to that dear old lady just down the road there.'

'Oh, you naughty story-teller!' said the big man, and he looked really shocked. 'You look quite a nice little fellow, too – and yet you tell stories and steal bags. It is really shocking. Do you want me to call a policeman?'

'I think you must be mad,' said Twiddle, holding on to the bag for all he was worth, for he felt quite sure the man would grab it if he could. '*I* shall call a policeman if you behave like this. I tell you this bag belongs to that old lady down the road there, and she left it behind in the grocer's – so I am running after her with it.'

'You do tell big stories!' said the man. 'Now look here – let's both go after that old lady, and if she says it's her bag, she can have it, and I'll say I'm sorry and go away.'

'Well, that seems fair enough,' said Twiddle, and they went after the old lady, who looked very surprised indeed when two men stopped her and spoke to her.

'Madam,' said Mr Twiddle, and he raised his hat very politely. 'Madam, you left your bag behind in the grocer's. Here it is.'

The old lady looked at it and seemed puzzled. She didn't take the bag.

'Well, here it is,' said Twiddle, impatiently, and held it out to her. She shook her head.

'I don't want it,' she said. 'It's not my bag!'

Twiddle stared at her as if he couldn't believe his ears. She pushed the bag away.

'I don't want it, I tell you,' she said. 'It isn't mine. I'm an honest old woman, I am, and I don't want things that are not mine.'

She walked on, looking quite haughty. The big, burly man looked at Twiddle.

'There you are!' he said. 'What did I tell you? It's all a made-up story of yours, isn't it? You saw the bag, picked it up, went off with it, and pretended you were taking it to the old lady when I found out you had it! I think you are a very bad fellow.'

'I – I seem to have made a little mistake,' said poor Twiddle, looking very hot and bothered. He gave the bag to the man. 'Really, you must not think bad things of me, my dear sir. I belong to this town, and everyone knows me. I am a very honest and harmless fellow.'

'Well, we'll see about that!' said the big man. 'I'm going to see my sister's best friend today – and I shall ask her about you, and tell her what you've done. Yes, this story shall go all round the town!'

'Who – who are you going to see?' asked

poor Twiddle, hoping it wasn't Mrs Gab, or Miss Gossip, for then surely everyone would know how silly he had been! Mrs Gab and Miss Gossip spread all kinds of tales about.

'I'm going to see Mrs Twiddle,' said the man, 'and a very good woman she is, so I believe. My sister has often told me about her.'

Poor Twiddle! He didn't know what to say. Then he cheered up. After all, Mrs Twiddle was his wife and she loved him. Perhaps she would stick up for him. She often scolded him for things, but she knew he was kind and honest.

He didn't say any more but trotted back to the grocer's shop. He found his list on the counter and gave his order. He waited whilst everything was packed up. Then he went back home.

Now the big, burly man was there before him, and had already told Mrs Twiddle about the bad, dishonest fellow who had taken his bag that morning. Mrs Twiddle was shocked. 'What was he like?' she said.

'Why – there he is – coming up your front path this very minute!' said the big man. 'You be careful of him, Mrs Twiddle. He may rob you, or deceive you with his tales.'

Then the big man got a surprise. Mrs Twiddle went very red. She looked as if she was going to burst. She picked up a broom and looked so fierce that the man was alarmed.

'You go out of my house at once,' said Mrs Twiddle. 'Saying things like that about my Twiddle, who is the dearest, best, honestest – yes, and stupidest – fellow that ever lived. Take your bag and go!'

Twiddle heard all this – and he saw Mrs Twiddle suddenly sweep with the broom at the big man's feet. He laughed. How he laughed. Then he caught hold of Mrs Twiddle and stopped her.

'Wait, my love,' he said. 'Don't send him away. I've been foolish this morning, and so has he. But it was worth it to hear you say all those nice things about me! Don't sweep the poor fellow off his feet!'

Mrs Twiddle laughed. The big man laughed, too. Twiddle laughed the loudest. He shook hands with the man, and Mrs Twiddle put the broom away.

'It's all turned into a good joke!' said Twiddle. 'Now you just come and look at my garden whilst Mrs Twiddle gets the dinner!'

Dear old Twiddle – he does get into muddles, doesn't he?

# Well, Really,
# Mr Twiddle!

# Well, Really, Mr Twiddle!

Enid Blyton

*Illustrations by Stephen Dell*

BLOOMSBURY
CHILDREN'S
BOOKS

# Contents

*Chapter 1*

# *Well, Really, Mr Twiddle!*

'I'm certainly in luck today,' said Mr Twiddle, looking very pleased with himself. 'First, I found that nice pencil I lost last week, and then when I went to feed the hens there were five eggs, and now the postman has brought me a present from my sister Hannah – a nice new hat!'

He tried it on. It certainly was a nice hat. Mrs Twiddle wanted to put a little brown hen feather in the band, but Mr Twiddle wouldn't let her.

'No. I don't like feathers in hats,' he said. 'If only I had a nice new suit now, to go with my hat. I *should* look smart!'

'Well, as you're having such a lucky day you might find one lying in the road,' said Mrs

Twiddle, with a giggle.

'You simply never know what might happen when your luck is in,' said Twiddle. 'I wouldn't be a bit surprised if I found a five-pound note when I was out walking this morning.'

'Well, you'd have to take it to the police station and hand it in to the police, and tell them to find the owner,' said Mrs Twiddle.

'Ah, but as my luck is in they wouldn't find the owner, and they would have to give it back to me,' said Mr Twiddle, still admiring himself in his new hat.

'You've got it on back to front, but I suppose you don't really mind that,' said Mrs Twiddle, with another little giggle.

A timid knock came at the door, and a little girl's head peeped in. 'Please, Mrs Twiddle, may I borrow your cat to play with this morning?'

'Certainly, dear,' said Mrs Twiddle. 'Call her. She does so love playing with a kind little girl like you.'

Mr Twiddle watched the little girl carry the purring cat away, and he looked very pleased. 'Well, if that isn't *another* bit of luck!' he said. 'We've got rid of that cat for a whole morning. Now I can walk about the house without falling over it.'

'I don't know why you don't like our dear old cat,' said Mrs Twiddle. 'You're the only person who ever falls over it, anyway.'

'And do you know why?' said Mr Twiddle, suddenly looking rather fierce. 'I'll tell you! It's because I'm the only person that cat tries to trip up! She's always walking through my legs! Bit of good luck, I tell you, Puss going off with Polly.'

245

'Well, if you don't go and get the fish for dinner your good luck will come to an end, because you'll go hungry,' said Mrs Twiddle, looking at the clock. 'Put on your old hat, Twiddle, and get the shopping basket, do. Take some paper with you for the fish.'

Twiddle fetched the basket. He put a newspaper in it to wrap the fish in when he bought it. But he didn't change his nice new hat for his old one. No, he thought he looked so nice in the new one that he felt he might as well give everyone a treat when they looked at him!

'Put your *old* hat on!' called Mrs Twiddle, when she saw him going out with his new one on his head.

'No, no, dear,' said Mr Twiddle, trying to find a quick reason for keeping it on. 'I told you my luck is in today – suppose I find a nice new suit somewhere. I'd look dreadful if I didn't have a nice hat to wear with it.'

'Don't be silly, Twiddle!' called his wife, but by that time he was out of the front gate and couldn't hear her. He hurried along to the fish shop.

He stood in the queue for ten minutes and then got a large piece of rather smelly cod.

He had it wrapped carefully in the newspaper, and hoped that he wouldn't be followed home by half a dozen cats.

'I won't go home through the village in case the cats smell the fish and come after me,' thought Twiddle, remembering how annoyed he had been last time by having five cats trailing after him all the way home, sniffing the kippers in his basket. 'I'll go back through the wood.'

So he took the other way home and wandered along in the wood, enjoying the smell of the hawthorn blossom and the sight of the bluebells. It was a very hot day, and Mr Twiddle was glad he hadn't got an overcoat on.

Then he saw a most extraordinary sight. He stopped and looked as if he couldn't believe his eyes. Neatly folded up under a bush was a suit of beautiful new clothes!

Twiddle stood and stared and his heart began to thump in excitement. There! What had he said that very morning! His luck was certainly in, because here was a new suit of clothes waiting to go with his nice new hat!

'But, wait, Twiddle,' said Twiddle to himself, cautiously. 'They might belong to someone, you know. Have a look around and see.'

So he had a good look round, but he could see nobody at all. He went back to the neat pile of clothes and looked at them. Coat, trousers, waistcoat, vest, socks, braces – why, there was everything except a hat!

'This is most extraordinary,' said Twiddle. 'It just shows what can happen when your luck is in! I get a new hat from Hannah – and, lo and behold, I find a complete set of new clothes to go with it, and nobody to own them!'

He looked at them again. They were exactly his size. They were *meant* for him! He looked at the collar of the suit, half expecting to see his own name marked there, and was quite disappointed when it wasn't. But, would you believe it, on the neat white handkerchief folded inside the left-hand top pocket of the coat was the letter T in pale blue thread! Twiddle stared in the greatest delight.

'That proves it,' he said. 'Absolutely. Completely. No doubt whatever. This certainly is my lucky morning! Goodness knows what I shall find next!'

He picked up the clothes and was about to put them into his basket when he remembered the fish. 'Better undo the fish, take a bit of the paper and wrap up the clothes in it or they'll smell of fish,' said Twiddle, forgetting that the paper must smell very strongly of fish already.

He wrapped the clothes up carefully in some of the newspaper, and then made his way home, wondering what bit of good luck would happen to him next. 'I shall put on this new suit as soon as I get home,' thought Mr Twiddle, 'and wear it with my new hat. How grand I shall look.'

He was longing to tell his wife of his new piece of luck, and he was disappointed when he got home and found that she was out. He went to get himself some lemonade to drink, and then heard Mrs Twiddle at the front door. She was talking to somebody.

'Bother! She's brought a visitor home,' thought Mr Twiddle, who didn't like his wife's visitors very much because they talked such a lot.

Then he got a terrible shock. Mrs Twiddle brought her visitor into the kitchen, and Twiddle could hardly believe his eyes when he saw a poor shivering, dripping man in a wet swim-suit! He gaped at him in surprise.

'Twiddle! I met this poor fellow running down the street in an awful state,' said Mrs Twiddle. 'He thought he would bathe in the Blue Pool because it was so hot today, so he took his swim-suit and went to the wood. He took off his nice new clothes, hid them under a bush, and went to bathe.'

'And w-w-when I c-c-c-came b-b-b-back, they had been t-t-taken by a r-r-robber!' said the shivering man, standing as close to the kitchen fire as he could.

'So, Twiddle, I brought the poor fellow in

here, and I thought you could lend him a suit,' said Mrs Twiddle, 'and I thought I'd give him a good hot meal, or he'll get a terrible cold, and then perhaps you'd go along to the police station with him and tell the police about the robbery. I mean, a man who is hateful enough to take a bather's clothes deserves to go to prison at once!'

Twiddle's heart went right down into his boots and stayed there. He stared at his wife in such a peculiar way that she thought he must be ill. He couldn't say a single word.

But he thought a lot! 'Oh, dear! So they were *his* clothes – and he was bathing! Why didn't I think of the Blue Pool? Oh, dear, oh, dear – I hope Mrs Twiddle doesn't look in the basket yet and find the clothes. What am I to *do*?'

Twiddle, don't stand there gaping like a moonstruck goldfish!' said Mrs Twiddle, sharply. 'Go and get an old suit of clothes, quickly. Do you want this poor fellow to die of cold?'

Mr Twiddle wasn't sure if he did or not, he felt in such a terrible muddle. He went upstairs to think it over, but then came down again very quickly when he remembered he had left the basket in the scullery with the fish and the suit there. He must certainly hide that basket!

He snatched up the basket, opened the scullery window and dropped the basket and its contents neatly outside under a lilac bush. There! They would be safe there till he could think what was best to do.

'Twiddle! What in the world are you doing in the scullery?' called his wife. 'You don't keep your clothes *there*! They're in the cupboard upstairs.'

Twiddle shot upstairs. He sank down on his bed. What could he do? What could he say? Nobody would believe him if he said he had thought that finding those clothes was just a bit of the good luck he had had that day. He could see himself now that it had been a very silly thing to think. But he really had thought it.

'If I go down and give him his right clothes, he might quite well haul me off to the police station and put me into prison,' thought poor Mr Twiddle. 'And if I don't give him them I shall feel really awful. He's got to have them back somehow.

Mrs Twiddle shouted upstairs: 'TWIDDLE!

*Will* you bring some clothes down at once for this poor shivering fellow? I'm just going to cook dinner quickly, so that he can have something hot. Where's the fish?'

*Now* Twiddle was in another muddle. The fish was in the basket underneath the lilac bush outside the scullery window. But he couldn't say that, of course. He seemed to be getting deeper and deeper into trouble. He scrabbled hastily in the cupboard and took down an armful of clothes. Mrs Twiddle gave them to the wet, shivering bather, and shut him into the sitting-room to change.

'Where's the fish?' she said to Twiddle, sharply.

'Er – now let me see,' said Twiddle looking very vague. 'Now – just let me see.'

A miaow suddenly came from the scullery next to the kitchen. 'There's Puss back again,' said Mrs Twiddle, and she looked pleased. 'Open the kitchen door and let her in, Twiddle. She's a real home-cat – never stays away for long!'

Twiddle opened the door, feeling that his good luck had completely vanished. The cat appeared, dragging behind it a pair of fishy-smelling trousers!

Twiddle stared at the cat with great dislike. He knew at once what had happened. That tiresome animal had come home, smelt the fish in the basket lying under the clothes, and had scrabbled about in the paper and brought in the trousers, because they now smelt so deliciously of fish.

'Well! Look at that!' said Mrs Twiddle, in the greatest astonishment. 'Whatever will the cat bring in next? A pair of trousers! Where did she get them from?'

The cat disappeared, and came back again dragging a coat, which also smelt very strongly of fish. Mrs Twiddle began to think she must be in some kind of peculiar dream made up of shivering bathers, fishy clothes and a cat that came in and out with them.

Then the sitting-room door flew open and out came the bather, looking very different in Twiddle's old suit, which fitted him perfectly. He stood still and stared when he saw his coat and trousers over Mrs Twiddle's arm – and then stared even more when the cat reappeared, dragging a pair of fishy socks.

'I say – look – they're my clothes the cat is bringing in,' stammered the man, in amazement.

'*Your* clothes? Your c-c-c –' stammered Mrs Twiddle, thinking that her dream was turning into a nightmare. 'But how could Puss find them? Oh, goodness me, now she's bringing in a vest!'

The man picked up all his clothes. Mr Twiddle forced himself to speak in an ordinary kind of voice, though he was trembling inside. 'Well – if they're your clothes, perhaps you'd like to go back into the sitting-room again, take off my suit, and put your own on.'

'No,' said the man, decidedly, sniffing at his

clothes. 'They smell of fish. I couldn't possibly wear them till the smell is gone. If you don't mind, I'll wear yours till tomorrow, then put my own on, I'll return yours then. I'll go now – but I wish I knew where your cat got my clothes from.'

He went out of the front door and banged it shut. Mrs Twiddle stared at Mr Twiddle, feeling rather faint. She sat down in her rocking-chair. 'Oh, Twiddle! I don't understand this at all. I feel quite strange. How did Puss get those clothes? Do you think she was clever enough to understand all we said, and went to hunt for them and found them?'

'No, I don't,' said Twiddle. 'It was just a bit of that cat's usual interference. She –'

Mrs Twiddle alarmed him by suddenly leaping to her feet with a yell. 'Look! The cat's got the fish! Is that the fish you brought home for dinner, Twiddle? Oh, she's stolen it – she's over the wall by now. Twiddle, where did you put that fish, you silly, stupid fellow?'

'It was in the basket – er – under the lilac bush,' said poor Twiddle.

Mrs Twiddle looked at him as if he was quite mad. 'Under the lilac bush! But WHY? Have you gone mad, Twiddle? You'd better go to bed, I think. You must be ill.'

Twiddle thought that bed would be a very nice peaceful place, and he went up very thankfully. There was no dinner because the cat had taken the fish, but Mr Twiddle didn't mind that. It was nice to be able to pretend to be asleep, and not be asked any more awkward questions. *What* a good thing the cat had found the clothes and brought them in, after all! Now nobody would ever know the silly thing he had done in taking them home himself.

But Twiddle is going to get a shock – because that bather isn't going to come back with Twiddle's old suit! He's a dishonest fellow, and he's going to keep it. But how can Twiddle go to the police and complain about *that*? Didn't he do exactly the same thing himself, when he thought his luck was in?

Poor old Twiddle! He's not so lucky, after all!

## Chapter 2

# Mr Twiddle Forgets

'Twiddle, it's the New Year tomorrow,' said Mrs Twiddle, busily darning an enormous hole in one of Mr Twiddle's socks. 'New Year's Eve tonight – the time when people make good resolutions.'

'What exactly is a resolution?' asked Mr Twiddle. 'It's such a long and peculiar word.'

'Well – when you make a resolution it just means that you resolve to do something and really mean it,' said Mrs Twiddle. 'Don't pretend you don't know that, Twiddle! You make a promise to yourself – you determine to do something; but if you make this resolution on New Year's Eve it's very important and very special.'

'Oh!' said Twiddle. 'Have *you* made any good resolutions?'

'Dear me, yes,' said Mrs Twiddle. 'I've resolved not to be cross with the paper-boy when he brings the wrong paper – and I've resolved to mend all those old shirts of yours I've been putting off for so long – and I've resolved not to let you snore at nights –'

'Well! What a peculiar resolution!' said Mr Twiddle, indignantly. 'Surely that ought to be *my* resolution, not yours?'

'Oh, no, dear – because *you* can't stop yourself snoring, and I very well can,' said Mrs Twiddle. 'I've only got to pinch you hard and you stop.'

'Well, I don't think that's at all a nice resolution to make,' said Twiddle.

'Now, now, don't be silly. You think about your own resolutions, not mine,' said Mrs Twiddle.

Twiddle thought, 'I've got quite a lot in my mind,' he said at last. 'I'll remember to chop the wood for you. I'll remember to mend that chair leg you've been asking me about for ages. I'll resolve to be kinder to the cat – though that will be hard because she honestly does try to trip me up on purpose, I'm sure of it – still, I'll buy her some fish to show her I mean to be kind.'

'Miaow,' said the cat, thrilled, and dug its claws into Twiddle's ankles as it stretched itself.

'What do you want to do that for, you unkind, horrible creature?' shouted Twiddle, and scolded the cat.

'Well!' said Mrs Twiddle, in surprise. 'I don't think much of your resolutions if you forget them so quickly.'

'I haven't forgotten,' said Twiddle. 'But I haven't begun them yet – it isn't New Year's Day till tomorrow. Now, let me think – I'll make a resolution to wind up the clock – and to paint the shed – and to sweep the kitchen chimney for you – and –'

'Now, Twiddle, it's not a good thing to make so many resolutions,' said Mrs Twiddle. 'Make *one* – one good sensible one – and keep it.'

'All right,' said Twiddle, 'I will. I know! I'll make a resolution not to forget a single thing! There – now you won't have to keep on telling me what a dreadful memory I have.'

'Splendid!' said Mrs Twiddle. 'Now you write down that resolution and put it somewhere to remind you – or else you'll forget it.

So Twiddle wrote out his resolution in his best handwriting. 'My New Year's Resolution is that I will not forget a single thing!'

He stood it behind the clock where he could see it. He felt very pleased with himself. Aha! He would show Mrs Twiddle that he could make just as good resolutions as she could!

Next morning he heard his wife up very

early. He called down in astonishment to know why she was up.

'Oh, just one of my good resolutions,' said Mrs Twiddle. 'I've determined I will never be late down in the morning. I hope you've remembered *your* resolution, Twiddle.'

Twiddle lay back in bed and thought hard. Now, what *was* his resolution? What could it have been? To be kind to the cat and get her fish? To wind up the clock? To mend something? Now *what* was that fine, sensible resolution he had made?

He fell asleep trying to remember. It was no use, he just couldn't think of it. He was very late down for breakfast and Mrs Twiddle was cross.

'Late the first morning of the year! And what about that good resolution of yours? Have you remembered it?'

Well, Mrs Twiddle was in one of her rather bustling moods, and Twiddle simply didn't dare to tell her he had already forgotten what his good resolution was. 'You just wait and see,' he told Mrs Twiddle.

After breakfast he tried again to remember what he had resolved to do. 'Was it to chop the wood?' he wondered. 'Perhaps it was. I'll

263

do it.'

So out he went and chopped a whole lot of wood for Mrs Twiddle. She was very pleased. But Twiddle didn't feel that had been his resolution. He tried something else. He stroked the cat and then actually went out to buy it some fish. But no – surely that wasn't his resolution? Mrs Twiddle didn't say anything to make him think it was.

Twiddle found the broken chair and mended the leg.

Now, surely *that* had been his resolution? Mrs Twiddle thanked him heartily. But she didn't say it was nice to see he had kept his resolution. So it couldn't be that.

Poor Twiddle! The things he did that day to try and find out what it was he had made a resolution about! He swept both the kitchen and the sitting-room chimneys and covered himself with soot. He had to have a bath, and he actually remembered to clean it after him – but somehow he didn't feel that had anything to do with his resolution either.

'I believe it was to paint the shed!' thought Mr Twiddle, and out he went to get a tin of paint and a brush.

Mrs Twiddle came out to watch. 'Well, you

really are good today,' she said. 'And how well you've painted the shed. Anyone would think you had made a good resolution to do it today!'

Oh, dear! So he hadn't made a resolution about painting the shed. Mr Twiddle felt very gloomy. How many more things was he going to do before he remembered what his resolution really was! If only he could ask Mrs Twiddle what it was. But she would laugh at him too much. No, he really must remember it himself.

He went in to wash for tea, wondering what else there was for him to do.

Wind up the clock! Yes, of course – perhaps *that* was his good resolution. Twiddle went to the clock on the mantelpiece and hunted for the key. Mrs Twiddle looked up.

'Reading your good resolution again?' she said.

'What do you mean?' asked Twiddle – and then he suddenly saw the good resolution he had written out so neatly the night before, and stood behind the clock. There it was, staring him in the face – 'My New Year's Resolution is that I will not forget a single thing!'

So that was it – dear, dear! – and the first thing he had done was to forget what his resolution had been! Whatever would Mrs Twiddle say if she knew?

'You've remembered your resolution marvellously, I think,' she said. 'Really marvellously! You haven't forgotten a single thing all day long, Twiddle. I do feel so pleased. I shall cook you a very special kipper for your tea!'

He did enjoy his kipper – but, you know, he didn't say a word to Mrs Twiddle about forgetting his resolution – not one single word. It's still there, behind the clock. I wonder how soon he'll forget it again!

## Chapter 3

# Twiddle Cuts the Grass

'I do wish,' said Mrs Twiddle, 'I *do* wish, Twiddle, that you would do something about that long grass in the garden. It looks so very untidy.'

Mrs Twiddle said this almost every day. Mr Twiddle sighed. He knew he would have to cut that grass sooner or later. Well, it was a nice day. He might as well do it and get it over.

'Very well, my love,' he said. 'I'll take the scythe and mow it down. Anything to please you!'

'Well, put your garden trousers on, dear,' said Mrs Twiddle. 'You don't want to spoil your nice ones.'

Twiddle went upstairs and found his

267

garden trousers. They were old, grey flannel ones and he liked them. They were big and comfortable.

He put them on and then took everything out of the pockets of his other trousers and put them into the pockets of his garden trousers. In went his money, his keys, his handkerchief and a little roll of string that he always kept in case he might want some.

Then he went downstairs to find the scythe. 'It may be blunt, of course,' he said to Mrs Twiddle. 'Then I couldn't start mowing the grass today.'

'Well, it isn't blunt,' said Mrs Twiddle. 'I had it sharpened last week for you. Now do get to work, Twiddle – you've been ages already getting your garden trousers on.'

Twiddle went out into the garden. It was rather hot. Oh dear, scything was very very hard work! He would soon be dreadfully hot! He took off his coat.

He walked to the long grass with the big scythe in his hand. Dear, dear, it certainly was very long! He felt the blade of the scythe to see if it really was sharp, and it was.

Now, just as Mr Twiddle was about to begin his work, the cat walked over to him, and rubbed against his leg in a very loving manner. Twiddle was not very fond of his wife's cat. It always wanted doors or windows opened for it whenever Twiddle was sitting down reading his paper.

'Go away, Puss!' he said, sternly. 'I'm going to do a bit of scything. You don't want your tail cut off, do you? Well, use your brains, then, and get away. Shoo!'

The cat rubbed itself against Mr Twiddle's other leg. Then it sat down and began to wash itself.

'Did you hear what I said?' asked Twiddle.

'Go away from this long grass. Right away. Surely you would not be silly enough to lie down and sleep in it just when I'm going to scythe it? Of course, I know that's just the kind of thing you *would* do!'

The cat immediately curled itself up in the grass and tucked its head into its paws. Twiddle stirred it with his foot.

'Now, what did I say? Go and find Mrs Twiddle! Go along!'

The cat uncurled itself, went a little way away, gave Twiddle a nasty look and settled down again. Mr Twiddle began to get angry. He ran at the cat.

'Shoo! Get away! Why do you always make things difficult for me?'

The cat decided that Twiddle wanted to have a game with it. It jumped up, crouched down, and ran at Twiddle's feet. Then it darted away into the grass and hid. Twiddle ran at it again. 'Shoo! *Will* you go away and let me get on with my work?'

Mrs Twiddle put her head out of the window. 'Twiddle! What are you doing rushing about in the grass all by yourself and shouting like that?'

'I'm *not* all by myself!' shouted back

Twiddle, indignantly. 'The cat's here. How can I cut the grass if she's darting about the whole time?'

He chased the cat all about the grass and at last it ran off to Mrs Twiddle, its tail straight up in the air. Twiddle, feeling very hot, panted a bit, and then lifted the scythe.

But just as he was about to begin his work he saw something lying in the grass, something bright and round. He picked it up. A ten pence! Well, that was a nice little find. Very nice, indeed. He put it into his pocket with his other money.

'It's a pity I can't find a bit more money,' he said to himself. 'If I could I'd pay a man to do this heavy scything.'

He cut a piece of grass – and then he suddenly saw something shining once more. He bent down – goodness gracious, it was twenty pence!

'Very strange!' said Mr Twiddle. 'Some-one's been walking in this grass, I suppose, and dropped a bit of money. Who's been trespassing in my garden? Well, it serves him right to lose his money!'

He lifted his scythe again, and then thought that he might as well have a look to see if there was any more money lying in the long grass. So he put down his scythe and began to look.

He soon saw five pence and two pence! Then he found another ten pence. Well, well, this *was* a nice surprise, to be sure! 'Thirty-seven pence altogether. Splendid!'

He began to look very carefully indeed, bending down and peering in the grass, parting the long blades hopefully.

'Another twenty pence! Well, I never! And here's fifty pence. Would you believe it! Why, this bit of grass is full of money!'

It was most extraordinary. He kept on picking up five pences and two pences, ten pences and twenty pences wherever he looked. He put them all into his pocket, feeling very pleased indeed. 'I shall get a man to come and do the scything now. Why, I must have picked up about a five pound's worth of money already. Very nice, very nice indeed!'

Mrs Twiddle looked out of the window again to see if Twiddle was getting on well with his scything. She saw him bending down, creeping here and there, then suddenly standing up to put something into his pocket, then bending down again and creeping about. What *was* he doing?

'Twiddle!' shouted Mrs Twiddle. 'What *do* you think you're doing? Surely you're not playing with the cat?

'I am not!' said Twiddle, standing up, looking rather hot. 'I'm picking up money.'

'Good gracious!' said Mrs Twiddle. 'Money! Whatever do you mean?'

'What I say,' said Twiddle, and bent down to pick up a ten pence. He held it up to show her. 'It's easy. I just look for it and I see it. It's all over this piece of grass. Wherever I go I find five pences and two pences and ten

273

pences and twenty pences and fifty pences. Why, here's fifty pence by my foot now!'

So there was. Mrs Twiddle hurried down to the patch of long grass. 'Really, Twiddle! I can't believe it. How could there be so much money in this grass? Where in the world did it come from?'

'Somebody must have dropped it,' said Twiddle. 'Somebody trespassing in my garden. Serves him right to lose it.'

He picked up a ten pence and put it into his pocket. 'I'm going to pay a man to do this scything instead of me,' he said. 'And if you'd like to buy yourself a box of chocolates, I'd be pleased to give you the money. And we might perhaps buy a chicken for our dinner.'

Mrs Twiddle looked very puzzled. She couldn't understand this money business at all. Twiddle wandered away a little and then picked up a five pence. 'See! I tell you wherever I go in this grass I pick up money.'

'Your pocket must be absolutely full of it!' said Mrs Twiddle. 'How much have you got?'

'Well, I've picked up dozens and dozens of five pences and ten pences and twenty pences and things,' said Twiddle. 'I'll show you what I've got.'

He put his hand into his pocket to get out all the money he had put there. He felt round his pocket and a frown came on his face.

'What's the matter?' said Mrs Twiddle.

'A most extraordinary thing,' said Twiddle, looking astonished, 'I can't feel even a five pence in my pocket! And yet I put dozens of coins there. Where have they all gone?'

'Let me feel,' said Mrs Twiddle, and she put her hand into his pocket. She felt around – and then she found a big hole at the bottom!

'Twiddle! You've got an enormous hole in that pocket. I really do think you are the stupidest man I've ever known! Here you go walking about with a hole in your pocket, dropping all your money out, and picking it up and putting it in your pocket again and then out it falls, and you pick it up all over again – and think you're so rich we can have chicken for dinner!'

Mr Twiddle stared at his wife in dismay. He felt the hole in his pocket. 'Have I – have I been picking up the same five pence and the same ten pence, and the same twenty pence all the time?' he said. 'Wasn't this grass full of money, then?'

'No, you stupid man! Whatever money was

here fell from your pocket – when you were chasing the cat about, I should think,' said Mrs Twiddle. 'And you kept on picking it up and losing it and picking it up – oh, Twiddle, I think my cat's got more sense in its head than you have. Wasting all the morning doing a silly thing like that!'

Twiddle was very upset. He picked up a twenty pence by his foot and absent-mindedly put it into his pocket. It at once fell out and appeared by his foot again.

'See! That's what's been happening all the time,' said Mrs Twiddle. 'Now, you listen to me, Twiddle – I shan't give you any dinner at all till you've finished cutting this grass. So, if you want to play with the cat or go on picking up your money, you know what to expect!'

And little Mrs Twiddle walked back to the house quite crossly. Twiddle sighed loudly, took his scythe and set to work.

What a disappointment – and how cross Mrs Twiddle looked. Then a thought came into Twiddle's head. He threw down his scythe and ran across the garden till he came to the kitchen window. He popped his head in and made Mrs Twiddle jump.

'Now, you listen to me,' said Twiddle, quite

fiercely. 'Do you know whose fault all this is?
Yours, yours! And do you know why? Because
you didn't mend the hole in my pocket! Aha!
Aha!'

Then, feeling quite pleased with himself,
Twiddle went happily back to the grass and
scythed hard till it was all cut. And you will be
glad to know that Mrs Twiddle had a lovely

dinner ready for him, and gave him a hearty kiss when he came in.

'You're a dear old thing, even if you *are* stupid!' she said. 'Now, don't you dare to say Aha! to me again, or I shall laugh till I cry. Aha, indeed!'

*Chapter 4*

# A Knot in Twiddle's Hanky

'I do wish I could remember things,' said Mr Twiddle in despair. 'I meant to go and fetch my shoes before the shops closed, so that I could go for a nice walk this evening – and I forgot.'

'And you can't possibly go for a walk in those old shoes you're wearing,' said Mrs Twiddle. 'Why don't you tie a knot in your hanky, or something, Twiddle, then you would see it and remember you had to do something?'

'Well, that's just what I *will* do!' said Mr Twiddle, and he took out his big red handkerchief and tied a large knot at one corner. 'There! Now, when I see that knot I shall know I must remember something.'

'What are you going to remember?' asked Mrs Twiddle, with a little squeal of laughter.

'Oh, dear me, yes – I forgot I had to have something to remember, before I tied a knot,' said Mr Twiddle. 'Well, I know – I really must remember to fetch my shoes tomorrow. I'll leave the knot in for that.'

So he left it in, and went to read his paper in the garden. Before very long he took out his red hanky to mop his head – and he saw the knot.

'Aha! The knot! Now that was to make sure I remembered something. What was it?'

But for the life of him poor Mr Twiddle couldn't remember what the knot was for! So he called his wife. 'Can you think of anything I said I would do, and haven't done?' he asked.

'Good gracious, yes!' said Mrs Twiddle at once, thinking of a whole lot of things. 'What about cutting the grass?'

'Oh, dear – did I really put the knot in my hanky for that?' said Mr Twiddle, with a sigh. 'Well, well – it's no good putting knots in if I don't take any notice of them.' So he got up, fetched the lawn-mower and began to cut the grass.

He was so hot when he had finished that he sat down on the seat to rest. He pulled out his hanky – and in it he saw the knot again. He had forgotten to undo it! So he thought it was another knot, of course. He stared at it, frowning.

'Good gracious! Now what's *this* knot for? he wondered. He called to his wife. 'Is there anything else I ought to do?'

'Dear me, yes! What about weeding the lettuces?' called back his wife, giggling to herself to think that dear old Twiddle hadn't undone the knot.

Twiddle got up. 'Well, I never! Was that what the knot was for in my hanky? What a memory I've got, to be sure.'

So off he went to weed the lettuce bed, and it took him till supper-time. He was really very tired when he went in.

After his supper he took out his hanky to wipe some crumbs off his waistcoat – and again he saw the very same knot.

'Look at that!' he said to his wife, who turned away to laugh all by herself. 'What's *that* knot for, I'd like to know?'

'You haven't filled the coal bucket for me,' said Mrs Twiddle. 'Would it be that, Twiddle?'

'It might be,' said Twiddle. 'Anyway, I'll do it. Oh, dear, what a pity I saw the knot!'

He saw it again just before he went to bed. 'Bless us all! Here's a knot in my hanky again!' he said to his wife. 'The things I have to remember! What can it be now? Is there anything important I must do?'

'Yes. Put the cat out, and then get her in again,' said Mrs Twiddle, getting ready to go up to bed. 'You always forget that, Twiddle.'

Twiddle groaned. 'That cat! I let her in and out all day long. She just does it on purpose. And yet at night, when I kindly open the door for her without her asking me, she won't go out. Puss, come along! Out you go!'

Mrs Twiddle had gone upstairs by the time Mr Twiddle had let the cat out and waited patiently for it to come back again. He went up and got into bed beside his plump little wife.

He took his hanky to put under the pillow – and dear me, he saw the knot again! Yes, the very same knot.

Mrs Twiddle was asleep. Twiddle couldn't bear to wake her. He stared at the knot and tried to puzzle out what it was there to remind him of. To fasten all the windows? To rake out the kitchen fire? To see if the larder door was safely shut? To – to – to – well, what *was* it for?

Poor Twiddle got out of bed, put on his dressing-gown and went downstairs to see if he could find something he had forgotten to do. But he couldn't. The doors were locked, the windows were fastened, the larder was shut, the fire was raked out. Then what could it be?

He went into the sitting-room to see if everything was all right there, and fell over the cat, which got between his legs in her usual annoying way. He fell down with a crash, knocked over a little table, and down went Mrs Twiddle's best fern!

Mrs Twiddle woke up with a dreadful jump. 'Twiddle!' she said sharply. 'Burglars! Quick, Twiddle!'

But Twiddle wasn't there. Mrs Twiddle put on her dressing-gown and went downstairs in time to see Twiddle pelting the cat with the earth out of her plant pot! She was very cross indeed.

'Really, Twiddle! Have you *got* to do this sort of thing in the middle of the night when

I'm sound asleep? The poor cat! And my poor fern! Puss, Puss, come to me, then. Naughty Twiddle, what was he doing to you?'

'*Well*!' said Twiddle, annoyed. 'I like *that*! Why don't you ask your cat what she was doing to me? Tripping me up on purpose!'

'What did you come down for?' asked Mrs Twiddle, crossly.

'Well – to see if I'd forgotten to do something,' said Twiddle. 'But everything seems all right. I'm coming to bed. But that cat isn't. Leave her in the kitchen, please.'

Poor Pussy!' said Mrs Twiddle, and put the cat down. They went up to bed together and took off their dressing-gowns. Just as he got into bed Twiddle saw his hanky on the pillow and stared at the knot.

'That knot again!' he cried. 'What's it to remind me of *now*, I'd like to know. I'll never put another knot in my hanky again!'

'You won't need to!' said Mrs Twiddle, with a laugh. 'You seem to keep the same one in all the time. You never undo it! Oh, Twiddle, you'll be the death of me one day, with your foolish ways. Now, you listen to me – that knot is to tell you to lie down, shut your eyes and go to sleep!'

'Is it really?' said Twiddle, blowing out his candle and lying down very thankfully. 'Well, well – to think I put a knot in my hanky to remind me to do something I could *never* forget to do!'

And off he went to sleep. But I wonder if he'll remember to fetch his shoes next day? Do you think he will?

*Chapter 5*

# Mr Twiddle Goes Shopping

'Twiddle, you are not listening to anything I'm saying!' said Mrs Twiddle, crossly. 'There you sit in your chair, reading your newspaper and not paying any attention to me at all.'

'But you were only talking abut your shopping, my love,' said Mr Twiddle.

'I know – but *you* are to do the shopping for me today, so I want you to listen!' scolded Mrs Twiddle.

'Aren't you going to make me out a list?' said Mr Twiddle. 'You always take a list yourself.'

'Yes, of course I shall make you a list – but you must listen to me all the same,' said Mrs Twiddle.

287

'Very well, my dear,' said Mr Twiddle, but he didn't listen. He went on reading his paper, and all that Mrs Twiddle said went in at one ear and out at the other.

Somebody came to the door and Mrs Twiddle went to open it. When she came back, she had Twiddle's hat and coat and scarf in her hands.

'Here you are, Twiddle,' she said. 'Put these on and go quickly, or everything in the shops will be sold. Hurry!'

'You always want things done in such a

hurry,' grumbled Twiddle, putting down his paper and getting up.

He put on his coat and hat and Mrs Twiddle tied his scarf round his neck. Then she gave him a kiss. 'There you are, grumbler. And here is your shopping list. Take the basket and be sure to bring me back everything on the list.

Twiddle put the list in his pocket, picked up the basket, fell over the cat, and went out. It was a nice, bright, frosty day. Twiddle walked fast because it was cold.

He looked at his list. 'Butter, Soles, Drops, Corn, Hooks, Cake,' he read. 'Well, butter is easy. I'll call at the grocer's for that straight away.'

He collected the butter. 'Soles,' he thought. 'Good gracious! Does Mrs Twiddle want soles for her shoes – or soles to eat? Goodness knows!'

He thought the best thing to do would be to buy a pair of soles at the fish shop, and a pair of soles at the shoe shop. Then whatever happened, he would be right. So that is what he did! Into his basket went the fish, also the soles to go inside slippers.

He looked at the list again. 'Drops!

Goodness gracious, what kind of drops? Snowdrops? Peppermint drops? Eye drops? Which did Mrs Twiddle say?

Well, of course, as Twiddle hadn't listened at all to what Mrs Twiddle said to him he had no idea which to buy. He decided to get some more eye drops at the chemist's. Mrs Twiddle had weak eyes and she sometimes put drops into them at night. She might have meant those.

On the other hand she might have meant peppermint drops, which she liked very much. Very well, Mr Twiddle would get those too! So he went to the sweet shop and bought fifty pence-worth of peppermint drops.

Then he suddenly saw a woman selling bunches of snowdrops at the kerb. Snow*drops*! Well, well – Mrs Twiddle *might* have meant those. So he bought a little bunch and put it into his basket.

What was next on the list? Corn? Ah, corn, that was easy. But wait a minute – did Mrs Twiddle want corn for her hens, or a corn-cure for that big corn she was always complaining about? Twiddle decided to buy both, then Mrs Twiddle couldn't possibly grumble at him.

So he bought a bag of corn, which was very heavy, and a bottle of corn-cure. What next?

'Hooks. Hooks! Gracious, what kind of hooks? Hooks and eyes – curtain hooks – or crochet hooks?' wondered poor Mr Twiddle. 'Can't be curtain hooks, because she isn't hanging up any curtains. It must be crochet hooks – or hooks and eyes. I'll buy both and after that I'll buy the cake.'

It was a very, very heavy basket that Mr Twiddle took home. He decided to ask Mrs Twiddle to read down the list to him, and then he would hand out the things she said – perhaps she would add a little explanation as she read them. She might say 'soles for our supper,' then he would know that meant the fish, and not the slipper soles, and he would hand out the right thing.

'Hello, Twiddle dear, what a long time you've been!' said Mrs Twiddle, when he went into the house. 'Have you got every thing? I do hope you have. They were all most important.'

Mr Twiddle hoped he had got them too. Mrs Twiddle wouldn't be at all pleased if he had bought the wrong things!

'Read down the list, dear, and I'll hand out

the things,' said Twiddle. Mrs Twiddle took the list and began to read. 'Butter, Twiddle – did you get it?'

'Here it is,' said Twiddle, and handed it out. 'Next, please?'

'Soles, Twiddle. I do hope the fishmonger hadn't sold out,' said Mrs Twiddle. That was a most helpful remark. Mr Twiddle at once handed out the fish.

'The drops,' said Mrs Twiddle. 'Had the chemist got them?'

'Ah,' thought Twiddle, as he handed out the eye drops, 'this is fine! What a good idea of mine to get Mrs Twiddle to read out the list!'

'Corn,' said Mrs Twiddle. 'Ah, there it is in that bag. What a lovely lot you've brought, Twiddle! The hens *will* enjoy themselves!'

'Easier and easier!' thought Twiddle, feeling very pleased. 'What's next?'

'Hooks,' said Mrs Twiddle. 'Did you get them?'

Ah – now Twiddle didn't know which hooks to hand out – the hooks and eyes – or the crochet hooks! He pretended to stop and think whether he had got them or not.

'Oh, don't say you forgot my hooks and

eyes!' said Mrs Twiddle. 'I *told* you I wanted to sew them on to my new dress tonight. Oh, Twiddle!'

'Yes, yes, I got them!' said Twiddle delighted, and handed out the little packet. 'And here's the cake. That was the last thing on the list, wasn't it?'

'How clever you are!' said Mrs Twiddle. She looked at the basket. 'Why, you've got lots more things there, Twiddle? Snowdrops! How lovely! Are they for me?

'Yes,' said Twiddle, beaming. 'Of course.'

'Oh, how kind you are. And what are

these?' said Mrs Twiddle, opening the bag. 'Peppermint drops! How did you guess I had none left? And, oh, Twiddle, you don't mean to tell me you remembered to buy a pair of soles to put in my old bedroom slippers! How wonderful!'

'Well,' began Twiddle, 'you see –'

But Mrs Twiddle cut him short and gave him a hug. 'Thank you, thank you,' she said. 'They're lovely and just the right size.'

She dived into the basket again. 'Oh, Twiddle, you've bought me a new corn-cure for my poor corn – and you've got some new crochet hooks for me, too. You are really very kind and generous!'

Twiddle felt so pleased. He had done better than he thought! Mrs Twiddle flew round him; and found his slippers and his pipe. She gave him his newspaper, and made up the fire.

'Now you sit down and have a good read!' she said. 'And I'll make you toast and dripping for your tea. You deserve a treat, you nice, kind man!'

Well, he did really, didn't he – and how he enjoyed it!

*Chapter 6*

# Mr Twiddle's Shadow

Mr Twiddle was very angry with the cat. He spoke to it very sternly indeed.

'Now you listen to me, Cat! You have a good home here and plenty to eat, and a nice basket of your own. And what do you do? You steal things out of the larder if the door is left open so much as a crack, and you . . .'

The cat turned its back on Mr Twiddle and began to wash itself, wetting its paws and rubbing them over its face.

'Turn round!' said Mr Twiddle, in a rage. 'Don't you know your manners? I'm talking to you. Stop doing that soap-and-flannel act of yours, washing your silly face over and over, and look at me!'

The cat didn't. It just went on washing

itself. Twiddle marched round to the other side of it and addressed it again.

'All right!' If you think you can turn your back on me, you're wrong. Now, just let me tell you the things you've done to annoy me today. I left the breakfast table for just one moment and what did you do? Jumped up and ate all my bacon. And you . . .'

The cat turned its back to Twiddle again and began to wash another bit of itself. Twiddle flew into a real temper and stamped his foot. He began to shout.

'Rude creature! You stole my bacon, you made me open the window twice – once for you to come in and once for you to go out – and you tripped me up in the passage when I was carrying the milk. You did it on purpose so that you could lick up the milk!'

The cat walked haughtily to the door, stood by it, miaowed, and looked round at Twiddle.

'Ha! Now you're ordering me to open the door, are you?' said Twiddle. 'Well, I won't. I've had enough of you, see? I shall not open another window or door for you all my life long!'

The cat sat down patiently by the door and began to wash itself again. Twiddle went on

muttering. The kettle began to boil on the
stove. Twiddle ran to take it off before it
dripped all over the place.

The cat ran, too, and tripped up Twiddle as
neatly as could be.

Down he went with the kettle and a tiny
drop of the scalding water went over the cat.
She set up such a hullabaloo that Mrs Twiddle
came rushing into the kitchen.

She was just in time to see Twiddle give the
cat a most resounding whack. She was
horrified.

'TWIDDLE! What are you doing to MY cat?

I saw you smack it – and oh, poor thing, it must have got its tail scalded by the hot water!'

'It's been licking itself all morning,' said Twiddle. 'What about *me*? I've scalded myself, too – look, on my hand. That cat tripped me up on purpose to make me spill the water. Yes, I smacked it – and if it sits and looks at me like that I'll smack it again!'

'TWIDDLE!' cried Mrs Twiddle, amazed. 'This isn't like you. You sound so hard and cruel.'

'I *feel* hard and cruel,' said poor Twiddle, holding his scalded hand. 'I hope I've done the cat a lot of good, giving her a good smack like that. For two pins I'd give her another.'

'Now, stop, Twiddle,' said his wife, getting very stern. 'It doesn't do her any good to smack her.'

'How do you know?' said Twiddle. 'You've never smacked her. I tell you smacking is what she wants. I tell you smacking will make a different cat of her.'

'Well, it won't,' said Mrs Twiddle. 'It will just make her hate and hate you, Twiddle. You're very unkind indeed. That poor cat will never go near you again.'

'Well, that will be a very good thing,' said Twiddle. 'All the same I still say that smack has done her good.'

Mrs Twiddle was cross with him. She put on what Twiddle called her 'haughty face' and he didn't like it a bit. 'She keeps looking at me as if I was something on the rubbish heap,' he grumbled to himself. 'Oh dear, how long is she going to keep this up? It will make me miserable.'

The cat didn't go near Twiddle. It kept round Mrs Twiddle and mewed pitifully. Twiddle knew it was just making a fuss. Mrs Twiddle gave it all kinds of titbits and petted it and fussed it till poor Twiddle nearly went mad. Had that smack done it any good after all? If only it had!

Mrs Twiddle was so cold to poor Twiddle all day long that he really couldn't bear it. He very nearly said he was sorry he had been unkind to the cat, and only just stopped himself in time.

Then an idea came to him. It was a very silly idea, but still it *was* an idea. Mr Twiddle put on his coat and hat and called to his wife.

'Just going to get an evening paper!'

And off he went. He bought the paper and

then he went to the fishmonger's, where he bought a pound of yesterday's fish. It wasn't very fresh and the fishmonger was rather surprised at Twiddle picking out stale fish. Still, he didn't mind selling it, so off went Twiddle, the fish under his arm.

When he got to the field not far from his home, Mr Twiddle began to act in a most peculiar manner. He stepped into the field, looked cautiously round to make sure no one was watching him, and undid the parcel of stale fish. He spread it on the grass and then stamped on it! How he stamped! He jumped up and down on it too, and he even wiped the fish paper round his boots.

'There!' said Twiddle, walking out of the field and leaving the stale, jumped-on fish behind. 'Now if that cat doesn't follow me round like a shadow all this evening I shall be very surprised! Ha! Mrs Twiddle said the cat would never come near me again – but she will!'

He went in at the back door. Mrs Twiddle was in the kitchen, sweeping up some crumbs. The cat was sitting haughtily in the scullery. It gave Twiddle a very nasty look.

Twiddle walked in boldly, and pretended to aim a kick at the cat. It caught a whiff of the fishy smell on his boots, and opened its eyes wide. It sat up straight. My, what a wonderful smell!

Twiddle walked through into the kitchen. The cat followed at once, sniffing eagerly. It came right to Twiddle's heels. Mrs Twiddle looked up, still with her 'haughty face'. She was surprised to see the cat following Twiddle so closely.

'Nice and cosy in here,' said Twiddle, amiably. 'I'll just hang my things in the hall.'

He went into the hall. The cat followed closely at his heels and came back at his heels, too, feeling excited. Twiddle had never smelt so nice before. Where *had* he been, thought the cat.

Twiddle walked through the kitchen and into the scullery, just to let his wife see the cat following him again. Mrs Twiddle said nothing, but she couldn't help feeling more and more astonished. She knew her cat. It was a touchy cat. Even a cross word made it sulk, and it never had liked Mr Twiddle, who was very free with his cross words at times.

'I'm just going to get the wood in for the morning,' said Twiddle, and he walked out into the garden. The cat followed him, almost bumping its nose into his heels.

'Call your cat,' said Twiddle, stopping so suddenly that the cat *did* bump its nose. 'It's better in the warm kitchen.'

'Puss, Puss!' called Mrs Twiddle. 'Come to me, Puss dear!'

Puss-dear took not the slightest notice. She began to purr round Twiddle, and even rubbed her head against his legs. Mrs Twiddle simply couldn't understand it.

'PUSS!' she called sharply. She didn't like

302

the cat not coming to her when it was called. The cat gave her a sour look, and went on purring round Twiddle.

'Oh well, if she wants to be my shadow, let her!' said Twiddle airily, and went to the wood-shed, followed by the cat.

He came back with the cat. He went upstairs and the cat went too. He went to wash his hands in the bathroom and when Mrs Twiddle popped her head round the door, there was the cat, almost sitting on Twiddle's feet.

Twiddle came into the kitchen with the purring cat. He sat down in his chair. 'Now,' he said sternly to the cat, 'I do *not* want you on my knee. I am still not pleased with you. Just remember that hard smack I gave you this morning, and behave yourself!'

The cat didn't attempt to jump up as she usually did. She sat down contentedly at Twiddle's feet, so that the fishy smell on his boots kept coming to her nose. She suddenly turned her head and began to lick his boots with her pink tongue.

Mrs Twiddle was ironing and watching all the time. She put down her iron. 'Twiddle,' she said, in a much nicer voice than she had spoken to him all day, 'Twiddle, look at that cat – it's licking your boots!'

'Yes, I know. It's learnt that I'm master at last,' said Twiddle comfortably. 'I told you that a smack would do it good. It knows it's got to mind its *p's and q's* with me now. Any more nonsense from it and it will get another smack.'

Mrs Twiddle didn't say a word to that. She was thinking very hard. She had never seen the cat so attached to Twiddle before. Why, Twiddle might be its best friend instead of someone who had scalded it and smacked it not very many hours ago! Could it be that Twiddle was right? Did it need a good smack sometimes?

She went on ironing. The cat licked Twiddle's boots a bit longer, then lay down on his feet and went to sleep.

Mrs Twiddle simply could not get over its behaviour.

'Twiddle,' she said, after a bit, 'there's a funny sort of smell in this kitchen, isn't there? A sort of fishy smell.'

'Nonsense, my dear!' said Twiddle at once. 'Drains, I expect. You're always imagining things.'

'I hope the cat hasn't had the fish out of the larder,' said Mrs Twiddle, and she went to look. 'If she has I shall give her a good smack!'

That was too much for Mr Twiddle. He burst into such a loud laugh that the cat nearly jumped out of its skin. 'That's right,' said Twiddle. 'I tell you, this cat is all the better for a good smack!'

He went out to post a letter, later on, not because he wanted to, but because he meant to show Mrs Twiddle that the cat would even go out to walk with him. It did, of course, keeping to his heels like a shadow again. Mrs Twiddle was most impressed.

Twiddle sat down again when he got in. 'Here are your slippers, Twiddle, dear,' said Mrs Twiddle, in a meek voice, when he came in. 'I've warmed them for you.'

Twiddle was about to take them when he remembered not to. It would never do to take off his fishy boots – the cat would desert him at once! 'Can't be bothered to put on my slippers,' he said, much to Mrs Twiddle's astonishment. Really, what with Twiddle's behaviour and the cat's, she felt quite bewildered!

'Now, listen. I won't have the cat wandering up into our bedroom tonight,' said Twiddle, sternly, when he and his wife were ready to go to bed. 'I'm tired of her sleeping on my middle. I can't think why she never sleeps on yours. She must stay down here in the scullery.'

'She won't,' said Mrs Twiddle.

'She will,' said Twiddle. He took off his

306

boots and took them into the scullery. He stood them by the door to clean them in the morning. Then he spoke sternly to the cat.

'Cat! Sit down there by my boots and don't stir from them all night long. Do you hear?'

'Miaow,' said the cat, obediently, and lay down as close to the fishy boots as she possibly could. Mrs Twiddle could hardly believe her eyes.

'I think you're rather a wonderful man, Twiddle,' she said, when they went upstairs. 'Honestly, I never saw the cat so well behaved – why, it was just like your shadow.'

'Well, just you be firm with it,' said Twiddle. 'And mind you back me up when it annoys me. Next time it trips me up and I smack it, you must smack it, too.'

'Oh, I think one smack would be enough,' said kind Mrs Twiddle. 'Well, well, to think of that cat adoring you all evening like that! Who would have thought it? I feel quite jealous!'

'Oh, it will stop bothering itself about me tomorrow,' said Mr Twiddle, getting into bed, 'and it will follow you around just as usual. You'll see!'

It will, of course, because old Twiddle will

have cleaned his boots and they won't smell fishy any more!

The thing is, he sometimes forgets to clean them, and if Mrs Twiddle happens to do them for him, *what* will she think of the fishy smell? Twiddle, be sure you don't forget!

## Chapter 7

# When Mr Twiddle Was Asleep

'I don't know when I've felt so sleepy,' said Mr Twiddle, yawning, one afternoon.

'You always do feel sleepy in the afternoon,' said Mrs Twiddle, bustling round. 'And you always say exactly what you've just said. Now, Twiddle, I'm going out to see old Mrs Tabbit. You stay here in case anyone comes to the door.'

'Right!' said Twiddle, pleased at the idea of a peaceful afternoon in front of the fire. 'Is anyone likely to come?'

'No,' said Mrs Twiddle. 'And, Twiddle, see that the door is kept shut, will you, so that the cat doesn't get in and wander round. She'll try to get my knitting if she can. She's been a naughty puss lately over that.'

'I'll be very pleased to keep the cat out,' said Twiddle, settling down in his chair and opening his newspaper. 'Nothing I should like better. The longer she's out the more I'll be pleased.'

Mrs Twiddle put on her hat and coat and said goodbye. 'Now have a good snooze,' she said. 'You really do look rather tired – been reading the newspaper too much, I expect! Goodbye, Twiddle dear.'

'Goodbye, my love,' said Twiddle, feeling very amiable indeed. Fancy having an afternoon with nobody telling him to do this, that and the other – and the cat forbidden to come in, too! Now she wouldn't be able to sit herself on his knee all the afternoon and dig her claws into him. Aha! this was wonderful.

He was asleep before Mrs Twiddle had passed by the window. She had a look in and smiled to herself. 'Poor old Twiddle – he really *is* tired today!' she thought. 'I do hope nothing disturbs him.'

She went on her way to Mrs Tabbit's. Half-way there she met Mr Screw, the carpenter. He nodded to her.

'You naughty man!' said Mrs Twiddle, playfully. 'You haven't been to do the lock of my kitchen door yet – and it *is* so difficult to lock.'

'Well, there, ma'am – if I hadn't forgotten all about it!' said Mr Screw. He was a great big man, with a shock of red hair and a big nose. 'I'm down right sorry. Look, I've got a bit of time this afternoon. I'll go right along and do it now.'

'Oh, that *would* be nice of you,' said Mrs Twiddle. 'Could you really? The only thing is – you'll disturb Mr Twiddle. He's asleep in the kitchen and really very tired.'

'He sleeps so soundly that he won't hear

*me,*' said Mr Screw. 'I'll be very quiet, ma'am. He won't know I've been.'

So off he hurried to Twiddle's house. He was soon there. He peeped in at the kitchen window and saw Twiddle fast asleep. He went to the door and opened it.

He examined the lock. Dear, dear, he hadn't got the right tools with him – and if he tried to do it without them he would probably make a tremendous noise, and that would wake up Mr Twiddle.

Mr Screw scratched his head. If he went to fetch the right tools, and came back again, he'd be late for his next job. What could he do? Perhaps he had better make a noise after all and chance waking up Mr Twiddle?

'No, I won't do that,' said the carpenter suddenly. 'I know a better idea. I'll simply take the door off its hinges and carry it home with me – do the lock there and carry the door back. It won't take me any time then.'

So, very quietly, he began to take the door off its hinges. The cat came and watched him with much interest. She hadn't seen a door taken off before. She was pleased. Now she could get into the warm kitchen and perhaps find something to eat.

'Miaow!' said the cat and rubbed herself against the carpenter.

'Sh!' said the carpenter. 'You'll wake Mr Twiddle.'

The cat didn't mind about that at all, and went on miaowing. But Twiddle didn't stir. He was fast asleep and dreaming a wonderful dream about a dish of fried steak and onions that never grew smaller however much he ate of it. He snored a little.

Soon the carpenter had the door right off. He lifted it up on his shoulder and went off with it. The cat shot into the room as soon as the doorway was empty and leapt on to Twiddle's knee, digging her claws into him as usual.

Twiddle woke up with a jump. He stared at the cat in anger. 'How did *you* get in?' he asked, exasperated. 'Door and window shut and yet you appear. Get down from my knee at once.'

'Miaow,' said the cat, and tried to rub her head against Twiddle's chin. That was too much. He put her down and shut his eyes again. 'I don't know how you got in, but you can go out the same way,' he said.

An icy draught blew round his chair.

Twiddle sat up and looked at the fire. Had it gone down while he was asleep? Why was the room so cold?

No, the fire was beautiful. He sat back again and shut his eyes. But a little wind lifted his hair at the top, where it showed above the chair. Twiddle was puzzled. *Where* was this frightful draught coming from?

He looked round his chair – and to his enormous surprise, he saw the empty doorway. The wind was blowing through and making the place as cold as could be.

Twiddle didn't notice that the door was gone at first – he simply thought it was wide open. He glared at the cat. 'Did *you* manage to open that door on your own, you maddening, tiresome cat?'

The cat said nothing but began to wash herself. Twiddle got up and went to shut the door.

But the door, of course, wasn't there. Twiddle stared as if he couldn't believe his eyes. He ran his hand round the doorway – no, there was no door at all. It had absolutely vanished!

'Well – I must still be asleep, that's all,' said Twiddle, bewildered. 'I'll go and sit down again and maybe the door will be back again when I next wake up.'

So he went and sat down again – but he was so puzzled that he couldn't go to sleep. He kept looking round his chair at the empty doorway, and shivering in the draught.

'Somebody must have stolen the door!' he said to himself at last. 'A thief must have crept up when I was asleep, and taken the door off – the wicked robber!'

He went into the garden and called his

next-door neighbour. 'Hey! Did you see a man carrying a door this afternoon?'

The neighbour stared. 'No. Why should I? People don't usually go about carrying doors.'

'Well, *someone* is going about carrying a door,' said Twiddle, suddenly feeling very fierce indeed, 'and what's more I'm going to find out who it is!'

He rushed indoors, fell over the cat, got his hat and stick and rushed out. He trotted into the town, looking everywhere for a man carrying a door. But there wasn't one to be seen anywhere. This wasn't surprising, because the carpenter was now busily mending the lock in his own workroom.

As soon as he had finished it, he popped the door on his shoulder again and off he went back to Mr Twiddle's house. By that time Twiddle was at the other end of the town, walking up the steps to the police station, looking very fierce indeed.

'What do you want, sir?' asked the constable there.

'Someone's stolen my door!' said Twiddle, and he banged his hand on the desk. 'I want it back!'

316

'What door?' asked the policeman, astonished.

'My kitchen door,' said Mr Twiddle. 'When I was fast asleep, too. Taken it right away.'

'Er – well – this is very peculiar,' said the constable, and reached for his helmet. 'I'll come with you and make a report, sir.'

Twiddle marched him all the way to his house. He went down the back path to the kitchen door. 'This is where the door was stolen,' he said, and stopped suddenly.

The door was back! There it was, fast shut, and looking very solid indeed. Mr Screw had put it back five minutes before and had then gone off again.

The policeman stared stolidly at the door. 'Are you playing a joke on me?' he enquired.

Mr Twiddle looked scared. He felt the door gingerly. It was real and solid – but when he had left the house it hadn't been there. Now it was back! He simply couldn't understand it!

'Er – very peculiar,' said Mr Twiddle, still staring at the door. 'It wasn't there when I left. Now it's come back.'

'Doors don't come and go like that,' said the constable, putting away his notebook. 'I don't suppose you took a good look, sir – the door must have been there all the time. 'Good afternoon.'

Mrs Twiddle came in at that moment and was most surprised to see a policeman going out of the back gate. She hurried up to Twiddle, who was still standing outside the back door, looking puzzled.

'Twiddle, what have you been up to? Why did that policeman call?' she panted.

'Well – er – it was nothing much,' said Twiddle, suddenly feeling that he didn't really want to discuss vanishing doors with Mrs Twiddle. He didn't feel that she would believe him. 'He – er – well, he just came about a door.'

'About a *door*.' said Mrs Twiddle, even more astonished. 'What door?'

She opened the kitchen door and went inside. The very first thing she saw was the cat playing with her knitting! It had rolled the ball of wool all over the place, and had undone half the jumper she was making. Now it was busy chewing her needles!

She gave a scream. 'Oh, you wicked cat! Get her out, quick, Twiddle!'

Twiddle was only too pleased. He grabbed at the cat, which dodged aside, and Twiddle

hit his hand hard against the dresser. The cat
fled out of the open door.

'You deserve to go out, too, Twiddle,' said
Mrs Twiddle angrily. 'Didn't I *ask* you not to
let the cat in?'

'I didn't let her in,' said Twiddle, sucking
his hand.

'Well, you must have done. She can't come
in through a shut door,' said Mrs Twiddle.

'She did,' said Twiddle. 'But wait a minute
– perhaps she didn't. Perhaps she came in
after the door was gone!'

'Gone?' said Mrs Twiddle, staring at Twiddle. '*Gone*? What do you mean – *gone*? Doors don't go.'

'This one did,' said Twiddle; 'I fetched the police about it. And when we came back, the door had come again.'

'Twiddle, dear, do you feel quite well?' said Mrs Twiddle, suddenly, thinking he must be going mad or something. 'Would you like to go to bed?'

Twiddle thought it would be a good idea. Then perhaps he wouldn't have to do any more explaining about cats and knitting and doors that came and went.

'I think I *will* go to bed,' said Twiddle. So up he went. Mrs Twiddle fussed over him like anything. She gave him a hot-water bottle, she brought him hot milk, she even went out to buy him a late newspaper. He was tremendously pleased. He really enjoyed himself.

He's never found out why the door came and went, because the carpenter didn't bother to tell Mrs Twiddle about it. Mr Twiddle would have forgotten all about it long ago, if it wasn't that he keeps meeting the policeman he fetched that day.

'Morning, Mr Twiddle,' the policeman says each time. 'Had any more trouble with your *doors*?'

Dear old Twiddle! I can't help liking him, can you?

## Chapter 8

# Twiddle Goes for a Walk

Mrs Twiddle bustled in just at teatime. It was a winter's evening, and already almost dark outside. She called Twiddle.

'Twiddle! Twiddle! Where are you? Have you got the tea ready as I told you?'

Twiddle hadn't. He had gone to sleep in front of the kitchen fire, and had only just woken up when he heard Mrs Twiddle come in. He was now scurrying round filling the kettle, putting it on the stove, and trying to get out all the tea things at once!

'Twiddle! Can't you hear me? I'm home!' called Mrs Twiddle, walking into the kitchen. 'Dear me – you haven't even got the tea laid.'

'Just ready, *just* ready!' said Twiddle,

banging the loaf down on the platter. 'You must be early, my dear.'

'No, I'm not!' said Mrs Twiddle, taking off her hat. 'I'm late. And I'm tired and thirsty. I suppose you slept in front of the kitchen fire from the moment I went out and shut the door to the moment I came back, Twiddle. And I suppose you haven't done a single thing I asked you to – not one!'

Twiddle fell over the cat and didn't answer. He glared at the cat. 'Did you do that on purpose, you miserable animal? How did you get in? You were outside when I began to get tea.'

'Oh, Twiddle – she must have got in through the bedroom window,' said Mrs Twiddle. 'And I *asked* you to be sure and shut it if it rained. You can't have shut it. Did you?'

As Twiddle hadn't even known it had been raining that afternoon he certainly hadn't shut the window. Trust that cat to give him away!

'And did you fetch in some more coal as I asked you?' asked Mrs Twiddle. 'Oh, dear – no, you didn't! The scuttle is empty. And did you take the clothes in off the line? Oh, Twiddle – they're still there. I can see them

flapping in the darkness. They'll be soaked
with the rain! And what about the dog? Did
you take him for a short walk?'

Twiddle hadn't done anything at all except
go to sleep. He felt very much ashamed of
himself. Dear, dear – he hadn't even *thought*
about the dog!

'Oh, Twiddle – I do think you are very, very
mean,' said poor Mrs Twiddle, sitting down.
'I've been busy all the afternoon nursing my
poor sister, and I did so want my tea ready
when I got home. I don't believe you love me
one bit. Not one bit. You haven't done a thing
I asked you.'

To Twiddle's horror she burst into tears. He hurried over with his big hanky, but she pushed him away.

'No! You don't love me!' she sobbed. 'I know you don't. You just went to sleep and forgot all about me.'

Twiddle felt very guilty indeed. He felt lazy and unkind and selfish and good-for-nothing. He tried again to dry his wife's eyes. But she wouldn't let him. Twiddle was very miserable.

What could he do to put things right? He rushed about, made the tea, cut bread and butter and put out cakes. He tore out into the darkness and brought in the clothes from the line. He fell over the cat again, and didn't say a word. He rushed upstairs and shut the bedroom window, because it was raining once more. He went out and got some more coal in. The cat went with him, very interested in Twiddle's sudden fit of hurry-scurry.

He nearly fell over her again. He didn't say a word but pushed her into the coal cellar and shut the door firmly. 'You'll be out of my way in there,' he whispered, when he had banged the door. The cat settled down on the coal and began to wash herself. She quite liked the coal cellar.

But still Mrs Twiddle wouldn't forgive poor Twiddle. She ate her tea in silence. She wouldn't look at him. It was really dreadful.

Twiddle couldn't eat anything, he was so upset. What else could he do to show his wife that he was very sorry? He sat and thought. Then he got up and took down his hat and coat. 'I'm going to take the poor dog for a run,' he said. 'I'll fetch him from his kennel.'

The rain was pelting against the windows, and Twiddle did hope that Mrs Twiddle would say no, he wasn't to go out in such a downpour. But she didn't. She just sat and drank her tea and wouldn't even *look* at poor Twiddle! So out he went into the rain and darkness, and made his way to the kennel.

Rain or not, the dog was very glad to see him. He would hardly stand still for Twiddle to put on his lead. In the end Twiddle dropped it on the ground and couldn't find it again in the darkness. Oh, dear! He really didn't want to go back into the house to get a torch to look for the lead. So he took a bit of rope and tied that through the dog's collar instead.

He set off with the dog in the rain. He hadn't got an umbrella, so he soon got wet.

He was hungry and thirsty because he hadn't had any tea. He was also very miserable. So was the dog, because he didn't think walks in the rain and darkness were much fun – and he didn't like a silent, unhappy master.

Twiddle soon came to the town. He came to a brightly lit little place called 'Tilly's Tea Room.' A nice smell of toast came out from the door. It made Mr Twiddle feel very hungry indeed. He knew this tea room. It was a place where farmers came after market to have tea and toast and new-baked ginger cake. Outside was a strong railing to which they could tie their horses, cows, a sheep or two, and dogs.

Twiddle decided to go in and have some tea and toast. He tied the dog firmly to the railings by his rope. 'Shan't be long, old fellow,' he said. 'It's stopped raining now so you'll be all right.'

Twiddle enjoyed his tea and toast and new ginger cake. Then he thought he had better be getting back because Mrs Twiddle might think he was out too long. So he paid his bill and got up to go.

It was pitch dark outside now. Twiddle wished and wished he had brought a torch.

He groped his way to the railing and fell over what seemed to be a pig, by its excited grunts. He felt about for his dog.

'Where are you?' he said, and the dog barked gladly. Twiddle undid the rope from the railing and set off home.

'Come along,' he said. 'We'll get back. I shall be glad of my warm fire and you'll be glad of your cosy kennel.'

He walked home quickly, glad that it had stopped raining. He took the dog to its kennel and shut it in, giving it a push because it didn't seem to want to go in. Then he went indoors, hoping that Mrs Twiddle was in a better temper now.

But she wasn't. 'Where's the cat?' she asked him. 'I can hear her yowling, but I can't find her.'

Twiddle remembered where she was – oh, dear, in the coal cellar! He went to the door and listened. Yes – she was yowling loudly. Then he heard another noise, too – one that puzzled him.

'Hiss-ss-ss! Hiss-ss-ss!'

'What in the world is that noise?' asked Mrs Twiddle, surprised.

'Sounds like a large snake, or something.'

'HISS-SS-SS-SS!'

'Whatever can it be?' said Mrs Twiddle stepping back quickly. 'Gracious – if there's an escaped snake in the garden I shall scream the place down.'

Twiddle was just about to shut the door when they heard another noise – a loud cackling, angry and fierce. Mrs Twiddle looked most alarmed.

'Why – is there a goose out in the garden with the snake?' she asked. 'Oh, Twiddle, dear Twiddle, I do feel frightened. Please do go and get the dog – he'll soon scare away any creatures that shouldn't be about.'

Twiddle was pleased to hear himself being called 'dear' again, but he didn't much like going out into the darkness among snakes and geese that seemed suddenly to have arrived from nowhere. The cat yowled loudly again.

'Let the cat in, too, wherever she is,' said Mrs Twiddle. 'Do go on, Twiddle. Aren't you brave enough?'

Twiddle didn't really think he was – but he didn't feel that he could possibly risk making Mrs Twiddle cross again, so out he went in the darkness, very valiantly.

He went to the coal-cellar and let out the cat, which flew past him and with a loud screech.

Then, hoping that he wouldn't tread on a hissing snake or bump into a fierce goose, he went to the dog's kennel. He thought that he would feel much better with the dog beside him. He opened the kennel door and called the dog.

'Come on, old fellow, come on!'

He felt a sharp pain in his hand and drew back, shocked. 'You bit me!' he said. 'You bad dog! You bit your own master! Come on out.'

But the dog wouldn't come out. Instead that peculiar hissing noise came again. Twiddle scurried away in terror.

'The snake's in the kennel with the dog – and the dog bit me!' he shouted to his wife. Mrs Twiddle was most astonished.

'The dog *bit* you!' she said. 'Our own dear gentle dog! I don't believe it. I shall go out at once with the torch and bring him in myself, snakes or no snakes!'

And out she went, shining the torch bravely in front of her. Twiddle followed her. They came to the kennel and Mrs Twiddle shone her torch in to see the dog. She gave such a loud cry of alarm and astonishment that Twiddle almost scuttled back to the house again.

'Twiddle! Look – what's this in our dog's kennel? Oh, TWIDDLE! IT'S A GOOSE!'

And sure enough an enormous goose poked out her head and cackled and hissed loudly at Mrs Twiddle. She pushed it back and shut the kennel door on it. She went back to the house with Twiddle, marvelling at the goose in the kennel.

'A goose! A *goose*! However did it get in the dog's kennel? And where is the dog? No wonder we thought there were snakes about when that goose hissed! Twiddle, did *you* put that goose into the kennel?

Twiddle was just about to say no, of course not, how could he – when a dreadful thought came into his head.

Could he *possibly* have untied a goose from that railing, instead of his dog? It had been so dark that he might have got the ropes muddled and taken someone else's goose and left his poor old dog. Yes – he remembered now – the goose had felt very soft when he had pushed what he thought was his dog, into the kennel. It must have been a goose.

He had brought back somebody's goose! Oh, dear, oh, dear!

'Maybe I brought back a goose instead of the dog,' he said. 'I stopped and had tea at a tea-room and tied the dog up outside. Now don't you say a word – I'll take back the goose and find our dog.'

So out went poor Twiddle into the rain and darkness again, pulling the surprised and angry goose behind him. How he hoped his dog was still there!

And at home Mrs Twiddle was staring angrily at the cat, who was lying on a clean cushion making it absolutely black with coal-dust from the coal-cellar! Her paws and fur were black with it.

'And where have *you* been, I should like to know?' she said. 'Sitting in the cellar again, I suppose? How many times have I chased you out of there? You bad animal! Out you go and get yourself clean in the rain!'

And when Twiddle came home with the dog he was met by the cat, flying angrily out of the door with Mrs Twiddle chasing it.

Twiddle was pleased. He never had liked his wife's cat.

'Bring the poor dog in and dry him. And dry yourself too, Twiddle.' said Mrs Twiddle in a kind voice. 'I'll make you some hot cocoa. That cat must have been in the coal-cellar again! Just *look* at my nice clean cushion!'

Twiddle looked, but he didn't say a word. He wasn't going to risk making Mrs Twiddle cross all over again by explaining how the cat got into the coal-cellar. It was nice to see her smiling once more. He and the dog could snuggle up peacefully together by the fire.

They did – and will you believe it, Twiddle is fast asleep again! And so is the dog.

## Chapter 9

# Mr Twiddle Gets a Surprise

'I'm just going out, my love!' Mr Twiddle called to Mrs Twiddle.

'Twiddle! Now don't you forget the fish for the cat!' called Mrs Twiddle, running to the front door. 'And pay the bill at the newspaper shop. And goodness, don't you want a basket for the fish? You know how you make your coat smell if you come home clutching the packet of fish to your chest!'

'Dear me, yes – I must have a basket,' said Twiddle. His wife ran to get it. When she came back she had his mackintosh with her, too. 'It's going to rain,' she said. 'You had better take this, too, Twiddle.'

Twiddle set off, his mackintosh over one arm, and the basket swinging in his hand. He

335

met Mr Grin and had a nice little talk with him. He met Miss Hurry, but she was gone before he could say more than 'Good morning'.

As he passed the cake shop a very nice smell of hot scones came out. Twiddle stopped and sniffed. 'I think I'll pop in and have a cup of hot coffee and a scone or two,' he thought. 'I really didn't have much breakfast.'

So in he went and chose a table. Soon he was sipping a cup of coffee and eating a whole plate of warm, buttered scones. Very nice, indeed!

He heard a noise outside and looked out of the window. 'There now!' he said. 'Mrs Twiddle was right – it's raining! What a good thing I've got my mac. It's simply pouring down!'

He paid his bill, picked up his basket, and went to get his mac from the peg nearby. 'Now, let me see – what did I have to get?' he wondered. 'What *was* it now? Fish for breakfast? Fetch the papers? Call at the cleaners? What shopping did I have to do?'

He struggled into his mac and went out into the rain. Bother! What was it his wife had told him to get? The rain splashed into his face, and he groped in his pocket for a handkerchief.

He brought out a nice clean one, still folded tidily. Nice Mrs Twiddle! She had even put a clean hanky in his pocket for him! He felt something else there as well, and pulled it out.

Oh, *good*! A shopping list! Now he didn't need to try and remember what he had to get. Dear Mrs Twiddle had written it all down and he couldn't possibly make a mistake! He heaved a sigh of relief.

He put his hand in the other pocket and

found his pipe there – and a small tin of his tobacco. How very, very kind of Mrs Twiddle. Mr Twiddle felt very loving towards her and made up his mind to buy her some roses. She was very fond of roses.

He lit his pipe and looked at the list of shopping. It was rather a long one – no wonder Mrs Twiddle had written it all out, instead of leaving it to him to remember! Ha – herrings for breakfast – he *thought* there was something about fish! Toothpaste – cotton wool – he must go to the chemist for those. And what was this?

'Nice big bone,' read Twiddle. 'That's a bit funny. Oh, I expect she wants it for soup. Sausages – well, I can get those at the butcher's too. And, dear me – a coal hammer! Well, well – does Mrs Twiddle expect me to break up those big lumps of coal? She hasn't said a word to me about it!'

'Chocolate cake' came next on the list. Mr Twiddle beamed. He liked chocolate cake, and Mrs Twiddle hardly ever bought one because, she said, they were too dear. And look at this – six crumpets! If there was one thing Mr Twiddle liked more than any other it was toasted crumpets for tea!

'No wonder Mrs Twiddle told me to take a basket,' he thought. 'Well, well – what a lot of shopping – but very nice shopping, I must say. Chocolate cake – crumpets – sausages. Well, I hope *those* are for supper.'

Twiddle went off happily, smoking his pipe. He must certainly remember to buy some roses for Mrs Twiddle now. After all, she was going to give him such nice meals, she deserved some roses!

He went to the fishmonger's and bought some herrings. Ha, he would enjoy those! He went to the chemist and bought his favourite toothpaste and nice big packet of cotton wool.

When he came out of the chemist's shop he found it had stopped raining, so he took off his mac and folded it neatly over his arm.

'Now to the butcher for a big bone,' said Twiddle, quite enjoying himself. 'And the sausages, too. Look at them, all looped round the front of his shop.'

He came out of the butcher's shop with two big bones and a pound of pork sausages. Then he went off to the ironmonger's and bought a really fine coal hammer. 'This will break up those big lumps of coal quite easily!'

he thought, and swung it up and down in the air.

'Now then, now then!' said a voice just behind him. 'You nearly hit me on the nose!'

It was Mr Surly, so Twiddle said he was very, very sorry, he was just trying out his coal hammer to see how it would break up big lumps of coal.

'You're lucky to *have* coal,' said Mr Surly. 'We've only got wood. And fancy having lumps big enough to break up! Where did you get them from?'

Mr Twiddle had no idea, and as he didn't at

all like Mr Surly, he popped into the shop that sold crumpets and got rid of ~~Mr~~ Surly that way.

He bought the biggest chocolate cake he could see and six lovely crumpets with holes in them that made them look just like flat sponges.

By this time his basket was very, very full, and he staggered homewards with it.

Last of all he bought three beautiful red roses. 'Red roses mean "I love you",' said Twiddle to himself, pleased. 'Aha! Mrs Twiddle will like those!'

He got home and went indoors. Mrs Twiddle was in the kitchen. Twiddle tiptoed into the sitting-room, got a vase, filled it with water and put the three red roses into it. He left them in the middle of the table for Mrs Twiddle to see. He called her.

'I'm in the kitchen!' she cried. 'Just baking a cake. Come in here to me, Twiddle.'

Twiddle went in with his basket. 'I've done all the shopping,' he said. 'Quite a lot, too, there was.'

'Oh, no, Twiddle dear – there wasn't very much,' said Mrs Twiddle, busy at the oven.

'Meow,' said the cat, smelling the fish and

coming over to rub herself against Mr Twiddle's legs.

'Don't,' said Twiddle. 'You make the ankles of my trousers all hairy. How many times have I told you not to do that, Cat?'

'I expect she smells the fish you've brought her,' said Mrs Twiddle, looking into her oven.

'Fish for the cat? You said herrings for breakfast!' said Twiddle, in alarm.

'I didn't!' said Mrs Twiddle. 'We've got kippers for breakfast. You bought them yourself yesterday. *Don't* say you've got herrings as well. Really, Twiddle! Did you pay the bill at the newspaper shop? I gave you the money for it.'

'Er – no. Dear me, that wasn't on the list,' said Twiddle, feeling muddled. 'Yes – I do remember your asking me now. But –'

'Oh, Twiddle! That's the second time you've forgotten to pay the bill,' said Mrs Twiddle, banging the oven door.

'Well, I remembered *everything else*,' said Twiddle. 'Here are the bones for soup – and the sausages –'

'Bones for soup? Are you mad, Twiddle?' said his little wife. 'I never said a word about bones for soup.'

'Oh, well – perhaps you wanted bones for that dog next door you're so fond of,' said Twiddle huffily. 'How was I to know? And you *did* say sausages – it was down on –'

Mrs Twiddle was now taking the things out of his basket in amazement. 'Bones – and pork sausages – and herrings. No wonder the cat was interested in your basket and came to make a fuss of you!'

She lifted out the chocolate cake and the crumpets. 'Goodness me! What in the world did you go and get these for? I *told* you I was baking cakes today! Twiddle, I really begin to think you've gone mad!'

She took out the toothpaste and the cotton wool. 'Ah look at these! You had a new tube of toothpaste yesterday – and, why all this cotton wool? Are you going to stuff a cushion or something? And TWIDDLE! Is that a coal hammer? Oh, Twiddle, you'll be the death of me! You know we haven't any coal – only a bit of coke and some wood!'

'Well,' began Twiddle, most annoyed, 'all these things were down on your –'

'Twiddle! You must have spent all the money I gave you for the newspaper bill on these things!' said Mrs Twiddle. 'It was my house-keeping money! It was very wrong of you to do that. You can pay for them all out of your own money!'

Twiddle was most alarmed. 'But I can't. I only have enough to . . .'

Mrs Twiddle burst into tears. 'Why did you get all those things? Now I shall never, *never* be able to trust you to go shopping again.'

There came a knock at the front door just then. Twiddle went to see who it was, feeling very gloomy indeed. A tall man stood there, dressed in a mackintosh. He beamed at Twiddle.

'I say,' he said, 'I'm very, very sorry – but I've done something so silly.'

Twiddle was very, very glad to hear that someone else could do silly things. He asked the man in at once. 'It's like this,' said the man, standing in the hall, 'I went to have a cup of coffee at the tea shop – and by mistake I took your mac when I went out. So I've brought it back. It had your name in it. Did you by any chance take mine? They are alike!'

Mrs Twiddle came out to hear what all the talking was about. She looked at the mac Twiddle had hung in the hall. 'Yes – he took yours!' she said. 'They *are* alike! Dear, dear – you men!'

'Good gracious!' said Twiddle, light dawning on him all at once. 'I smoked your pipe, then – and used your hanky – and oh, my word, I bought all the things on your shopping list!'

'No! Did you really?' said the tall man. 'You know, I tried to remember everything that was down, but I couldn't. I bought the chocolate cake and the crumpets – and I bought the bones for soup, and the sausages and the herrings. Was there anything else on the list?'

'Yes – toothpaste – cotton wool – and a coal hammer,' said Twiddle dolefully.

'My word!' said the man. 'I forgot all those. I *shall* get into trouble when I get back home. But do you *want* toothpaste and cotton wool and a coal hammer?'

'Of course not!' said Mrs Twiddle, answering for Twiddle. 'You can have them if you'd like to pay us for them.'

'Oh, I will, with pleasure,' said the man. 'It will save me going back to the shops. Dear, dear – I must have the worst memory in the world.'

'Yes – even worse than mine,' agreed Twiddle happily 'Here's the hammer – tooth-paste – and cotton wool.'

'I'm sorry you bought the other things,' said the man, paying out the money. 'But I've bought them, too, and I really couldn't face my wife with *two* chocolate cakes, *two* lots of sausages, *two* –'

'No, no, of course not,' said Twiddle, who was not at all anxious to hand over the cake, the crumpets and the rest.

The man took off Twiddle's mac, and Twiddle gave him the right one. They said goodbye, and out he went, his basket full.

Mrs Twiddle still looked very cross. Twiddle knew she had a lot more to say.

'Come into the sitting-room, Twiddle,' said Mrs Twiddle, in a stern voice. 'I have something to say to you.' He followed her in, feeling very gloomy. She suddenly saw the three red roses in the vase.

'Wherever did those lovely flowers come from?' said Mrs Twiddle, and sniffed them in delight.

'I bought them for you,' said Twiddle, in a small voice.

'Red roses mean "I love you,"' said Mrs Twiddle, her eyes shining.

'That's why I bought them,' said Twiddle. 'I may be a very silly husband, but I do think you are a nice wife. So I bought you those roses.'

'Twiddle, you're a darling!' said Mrs Twiddle, and she gave him a very sudden hug. 'Now, when would you like the sausages? For supper? And I'll make some nice soup with those bones. And herrings will do fine for breakfast, because the kippers will keep. And we'll have a little tea party with those lovely crumpets and chocolate cake!'

Well, well, well! Twiddle simply couldn't

understand the sudden change. But I can, can't you? After all, if somebody loves you very much, you can put up with quite a lot of silliness! Dear old Twiddle, I can't help liking him.